DO NO HARM

DO NO HARM
and other stories

Gary McLouth

ACKNOWLEDGMENTS:

Ganado Dreaming previously published
Minnetonka Review #4, Minneapolis, MN (2009)

Cover and book design by Melissa Mykal Batalin
Cover painting by Ginny Howsam Friedman
Sketches by George Ulrich
Author photo by Jackie Pierce

Printed in the United States of America

The Troy Book Makers • Troy, New York • thetroybookmakers.com

To order additional copies of this title, contact your favorite local
bookstore or visit www.tbmbooks.com

ISBN: 978-1-61468-046-8

dedicated to
Dr. Sydney L. McLouth
1915 - 2006

These stories emerge from long term collaboration with my father. As story tellers we came from different disciplines. The doctor is ever conscious of confidentiality as he pursues factual histories that lead to particular diagnoses. The poet explores the esoteric, the dramatic, and the emotional aspects of human nature so that he might craft and tell stories to the public. Ironically, the tension between these two value systems led to my development as a fiction writer, because Dad, the doctor, coded his provocative stories so that persons, places, and often, things, had wisdom attached but very little in the ways of identification.

From an early age I became an attentive observer and listener. We spent a lot of time together, and apart, before our different perspectives blended into what I can only refer to as a persistence of vision and voice. Of course, if we had not loved, trusted and admired each other, the vision and voice thing wouldn't have happened.

Collaborating on stories mostly meant that we each had a devoted first listener. My greatest satisfaction and joy came from hearing Dad's approval at what I'd done with our material. In fact, I know that without me, many of his stories would have remained untold. And, I think he knew that without me, the stories would have lacked depth and dimension.

Since Dad's death in late 2006, I've endured his loss in ways I am continually coming to understand. Finding his voice —and employing his voice as fully as I do—lends my own voice confidence. In these stories, you may hear my father's voice in mine and mine in his. Neither of us intended that affect as a product of our collaboration, but as an expression of our familial and interpersonal ties, I now see the blending of those voices as inevitable.

Dad randomly seasoned his conversation with truisms that could strike you as non-sequiturs, at first.

It's a long road that doesn't turn, is one of my favorites. Dad delivered this one with a particular degree of relish, and the more I think about it, the better I know the road he's talking about.

Gary McLouth
Blue Mountain Lake, NY
2011

HOUSE CALL

Dr. Sydney L. McLouth

Summer in the country
long, lazy, humid afternoon
a slow ride down a narrow dusty road

Grain gorgeously ripe
undulating in the sun
proud, as if aware of its stature and beauty

On a mission
undesirable and unavoidable
I spare myself the moment a bit longer

Beautiful grain!

But the car continues
without much help on the gas pedal
and suddenly it seems
the old Smith place appears

Car turns into the driveway
as if it knew the way
and well it should – after thirty years

And now to the business at hand
How to tell Bill Smith
the diagnosis he and I dreaded

So, out of the car
black bag in hand
along the path by the deep well pump
past the arbor and barking dogs

Slowly, along the walk, onto the porch stairs
I hesitate at the screen door, the rusty latch
another welcome delay

But there on the porch in the old swing
lies Bill Smith
a wise and slight smile on his face

In my usual best effort at bedside manner
to put patient and friend at ease
to delay perhaps, the bad news, I blurt

"Have you got all your oats in, Bill?"
He replies with a sad grin,
"All the wild ones."

"I saw you way down the road;
You're not much of a faker, Doc.
That's got to be your slowest run by here
Since you stopped using horses."

"GOOD MEDICINE"
by Paul McComas

I first met the author of this book in April 2008 at the annual New York Writers Roundtable conference in Manhattan. The walrus-mustachioed and gregarious Gary came over to me following a panel on which I'd sat, introduced himself (in that distinctive upstate accent), and expressed appreciation for something I'd said about the importance of a writer focusing on his or her "characters and craft" rather than on market niches, financial recompense, or the prospect of fame. (An easy case, by the way, for a nicheless, under-compensated, less-than-famous writer like yours truly to make!)

Three days later, at Gary's invitation, I was his guest at a TV studio in Albany, where I came to know him as the affable and astute host of the Ion cable network's "Authors & Poets" show. I recall my interviewer praising the "multi-layered characterization" in my then-recently-published comedic coming-of-age novel Planet of the Dates, which he'd just finished reading—and which had just been optioned in Hollywood. This latter development gave Gary pause:

"Y'know," he commented on air, "a lot of writers are consciously trying to write so that their stuff will be picked up by Hollywood. I'm not so sure that's healthy. I work with students, and they're always asking, 'What should I do with this? What

I really want is to make a movie; I want to be famous'—and they're like twenty years old. And you're trying to explain to them, 'Well, uh, this sentence doesn't work!'"

Nodding, I burst into laughter. And thought: Aha! Kindred spirit!

After I'd concluded my East Coast tour and returned to my own teaching work back in Chicago, Gary and I kept in touch sporadically; all such correspondence bore out my early impression of kinship, shared values, and common purpose—literary and otherwise.

Still, none of this prepared me for the experience of reading—twice, in succession—the book in your hands.

Do No Harm and Other Stories is a landmark. Not only is this deceptively slim volume the best short-story collection I've read in several years; it also represents, at least to my mind, the long-overdue return of what I can only call "the Steinbeckian sensibility" to English-language fiction.* Lennie and George from Of Mice and Men would find, in these pages, a welcome home, if not necessarily a sanctuary from the world's evils. So would the disaffected yet good-humored laborers of Cannery Row and the breast-fed starving man from The Grapes of Wrath. If you're looking for Faulkner or (God knows why) James Joyce, or for postmodern too-cool uber-irony, then look elsewhere; you won't find anything showy, obscure, inaccessible, pretentious, or clever-to-a-fault in McLouth's work. (Or, for that matter, in mine. Again: Kindred spirit!)

What you will find in *Do No Harm* are eight stories and one near-novelette (the title—and standout—piece) that address—unflinchingly, with a full and open heart—the pleasures

---

* I don't mean to imply that McLouth is the only fiction writer today following, generally speaking, in Steinbeck's footsteps; so are Tony Earley, Alice Sebold, John M. Daniel, Joyce Carol Oates (in her own darkly brilliant, oft neo-gothic way), and many others—of which I hope I'm one. Rather, I view Gary as a member in good standing of what is, to me, a still-nascent but most welcome trend.

and perils, boons and banalities, challenges and chimeras of what it means to be human.

Society's have-nots constitute a sizable contingent of this book's characters. Why? Because this author, in the end, is each of his well-intentioned male protagonist/narrators—or was, at least, while writing them: Ben, the humble, noble country doctor who relates the book's four even-numbered tales (and who views his career as "helping people jump from pond to pond until they run out of water"); the committed and semi-tormented fiction writer of the first piece, "Conversation" (whose dilemma is resolved, in a sense, by all of the stories that follow); the observant, thoughtful grandson of "Cousin Henry"; the morally challenged yet (as if in compensation) brutally honest and self-critical high-school teacher of perhaps the book's most challenging piece, "A Life of the Mind"; the young rebel-wannabe turned middle-aged realtor of "What I Want to Say"; and the youthful mission worker of "Ganado Dreaming." The oft-struggling secondary characters in these stories really matter to these five narrators because, well, they matter to McLouth. And because these people matter to McLouth—and because he's a master tale-teller—they matter to us, the reader, as well.

Oh, and when Gary's funny, which is often, he is very funny!

On a personal note, I'll add that Gary's sensitivity to the trials of Native Americans in recent/ contemporary America (in both "What I Want to Say" and "Ganado Dreaming") not only touched me, but also gave me new insight into that particular branch of my own family tree. His are some of the truest, best-rounded "Indians" ever written. Likewise for the elderly African-American title character of "Artie's Place." It's important for writers like Gary (and me) who were born into multiple "areas of cultural privilege"—white, straight, male,

American, Christian, and living above the poverty line—to extend privilege to others by imbuing our craft with empathy and presenting minority characters who, while not idealized, demand the reader's respect.

Sprinkled throughout these nine stellar prose pieces are poetic flourishes and pithy home truths ranging from the lovely (train whistles that make "a symphony of night music, keeping time across the sleepy countryside") to the heart-breaking ("[I knew] the night would come when my [dying] brother's window would be dark, but I've kept his light on inside me all these years since") to the wry ("Nothing mysterious about what [Mom] was thinking: her thoughts and observations were hooked up to her mouth.") Exactly how pervasive are such tasty "morsels"? Well, the three I've cited all derive from just one story!

As does this—from the same piece, the title story "Do No Harm"—in what is perhaps the best moment in this consistently fine book's strongest story. The section below follows the critical injury of a young friend of "Doc" Ben's college-age son, Dan, which has plunged Dan into "an edgy existentialism":

> Over time, [Dan's] fatalism gave way to renewed faith and exuberance—for poetry and literature, as it turned out. He liked stories where love and loyalty endured tragedy and loss. I could see Dan's trust turning toward language and the expression of emotion impossible for him through any other means. When my friends ask me how he is and what he's doing now, I say Danny's a poet, and their faces brighten in wonder. . . . I guess a lot of doctors want to be writers. I'll bet a lot of writers would like to be doctors, too. . . . We refer to the practice of medicine as an art. Maybe for Dan, the

practice of art is a kind of medicine, and we're both working away at the same candle from either end. I doubt we'll make it to the middle, but the candle's burning shorter.

Well said, Ben—and Gary, too! Indeed, so well said that I quoted it in my recent eulogy for a dear friend (and devoted, art-loving physician), Dr. Sheldon Miller, for whom the practice of medicine—specifically, addiction psychiatry, which he co-founded as a recognized subspecialty—was an art. . .one through which he not only "did no harm," but did much good indeed.

With *Do No Harm and Other Stories*, McLouth, though "burning the candle from the other end" as did Shel, is likewise doing good. Gary, I take it, is Danny, for the former's own "practice of art," administered here in nine potent doses, serves as much-needed medicine—not only for the writer himself but, crucially, for this ailing world.

Paul McComas
Author of *Unforgettable*,
Planet of the Dates,
and *Unplugged*
Evanston, IL, October 2011

CONTENTS

CONVERSATION

"The guy's got a problem. I don't know what it's called, I'm sure there's a diagnostic category in the latest DSM. He rapes women. Sometimes he ends up killing them, maybe that's part of his thing, I don't know. He's really a stock character. Jack the Ripper, the Chainsaw Murderer, The Greenway Killer. Not really a fully developed character but the driving force in the story, the fear element that draws the other characters together.

"So, you put yourself in the mind of a rapist?"

"Yeah, more or less, I mean, to write him I have to be him. Think how he thinks, you know, feel how he feels, see the world through his eyes, so, sure, I have to know him, probably better than I want to."

"I don't think I like that."

"I don't either, like it."

"No, I mean like the fact that you're thinking like that. Him."

"It's just a character; that's how it works."

"It's a he, and he's you, and okay, but, not okay."

"Make some sense, for Christ's-sakes."

"You make me uncomfortable."

"You look pretty comfy to me."

"Talking to you, the person. You, the writer? Not so comfortable."

BEFORE

He watched her crossing the plaza on a warm autumn afternoon. The deep blue of the sky and the light movement of breeze through the Linden trees inspired him to slide away from the streetside café and walk toward the corner. On the short walk to intercept her he counted on his first impulse to meet her, to be followed by a second impulse which would have him say the right thing. He had no idea what would happen next.

She didn't spot him until they'd nearly bumped, and both stopped amid clumsy apologies. That's when he asked if she always closed her eyes while crossing the street, to which she said not always, to which he said she'd be more careful if he could buy her a Champagne cocktail to which she said that would actually be reckless and irresponsible of her in addition to exercising poor judgment, and so, yes.

The promise of an intense sexual relationship segued into a kind of simpatico arrangement to meet at this same downtown café after a long week of work days during which they both spent psychological and physical energy gathering data, analyzing data and distributing data. That's what she thought, but the day of a writer was not like the day of an insurance adjuster. She was who she was who she was, but what he thought about and how he thought about it might change him, making him who he created all day, thought like, sounded like, saw the world through the eyes of, like, then who was he at the end of the day? She asked him about it the first time, meaning to be casual, like making a joke. When he answered with a squint of concentration, a chill ran through her whole body even though they sat under the full sun.

NOW

"There's a woman, middle aged, attractive, alone in a wilderness park. She's left her cell phone in her a car, takes a short walk along one of the trails but follows a side path that leads her to a cliff overlooking a deep lake. It's a pastoral scene but something's foreboding about it. What is she thinking? How does she appear from a distance?"

She senses his distraction, hears a reaching for the rapist in his thin voice. She wishes she were elsewhere.

He sees the glint in her eyes about the same time she feels the tears. How he thinks about being a rapist must upset her, so he spreads his napkin across his lap, signals the waiter, and talks about another story he's contemplating about a woman who leaves her husband to meet an old boyfriend in Sao Paulo.

"You just came up with that for my benefit, or is it something you've been working on?"

"See? Just how my mind goes. Do you think it's worth anything, makes a story somehow?"

"You're asking me?"

"You're the reader, aren't you? What keeps you reading?"

"I don't know why I'm still talking to you."

What she feels like saying, but doesn't is that he is fooling around with her and she doesn't like it, but if she says it, he might shut up and never talk to her again. "I have to go, now." She fidgets with her purse strap. "I've got things to do. I'm late, late."

"That's another story," he says.

THE STORY

In the story, the woman watches the sun slip in and out of fleeting clouds as the afternoon passes. The surface of the water below her changes from blue to silver to a faint green to slate black swirled milky by reflections of cumulous clouds.

The rapist has not become the rapist yet. He sits on a ledge above the lake, and from his vantage point he can observe the woman. She is silhouetted against the airy space above the lake. Tall pines make deep shadows on the distant shore. How is it that his desire to rape her kicks into gear? Does he start out with that as his primal instinct; does she unconsciously contribute something to the situation that causes him to act? Where do I have to go, whom do I need to interview, how much do I have to read about the psycho-history of rape? These are the questions corkscrewing the writer's mind.

LATER

He keeps his midmorning routine, stopping by the café for coffee and a cinnamon scone. If it's sunny, he sits at a small table just under the awning outside where the traffic provides a bundle of background for his imagination, already greased by hours of writing. He allows himself to wonder when and how she will appear next while keeping the picture of her crossing the street that first time agile in his memory. She, crossing double lanes, wary of vehicles from either direction, looking from her left to her right and back to her left again in a tick-tock swinging of her head. He pictures, as if for the first time, the exposed nape of her neck, a flash of gold chain-link necklace disappearing into the warm seclusion of her cotton sweater. How did he know 'warm' or 'cotton'? He couldn't have known in that moment, could he, the experience of her.

"What are you writing, now?" she asks, wanting to hear him talk, but she can't resist a jab: "The rapist get his rocks off?"

"How nice to see you." He gives her a long look. "I had to put that one away, a while ago."

She sits across from him. Their eyes meet briefly; she looks away, first turning her head both ways as if checking the street. She notices his stubble-rough chin.

"Does that mean you couldn't imagine yourself going through with it?"

"The character couldn't. I guess that particular spark didn't ignite for him."

"Same difference, isn't it?"

He meets her comment with a long, puzzled stare and rotates his head in tight little circles, stretching his neck. "I don't see what you mean."

"But, isn't it?" She gathers her gloves and slides up and out of the patio chair. Before she turns down the walk she squeezes his shoulder.

"I didn't realize it was cold enough for gloves," he says.

FINALLY

He looks for her every day and waits another month before she reappears, sitting suddenly across the small round table. She's cut her hair so that it turns up above her shoulders. He isn't sure she hasn't streaked it lightly. She's not as he remembers until he hears her voice.

"How's the writer?"

"I don't know," he laughs, sadly.

"If you don't, who does?"

"Good question. I've been thinking about him a lot lately, the writer."

"And…"

"What he's writing about and why. There's just as dramatic a side to life that he actually knows about, so maybe he'll write about that. And, what have you been up to?"

"Thinking about you."

"You're teasing."

"No, actually not. I've decided to like you despite my doubts. The writer and the person, hands touching."

"I don't know what to say."

"It'll come to you."

DO NO HARM

When I first came to this town, I roomed down the street with Lydia Doyle. She put me up in the back bedroom, and late at night the trains sounded like they'd come right through the wall of the house. It's been a long time since I had any trouble sleeping and even now I can roll over and be asleep, in a couple of minutes, but sometimes my memory is restless and I enjoy revisiting old friends.

How a guy from one small, floundering town could travel up the road to another town not much different, if even a little worse off, and meet a girl like Marj and make a medical practice almost all at once and be plugging away at love and life these many years later is simply amazing to me. When I think about it, all I can say is that I'm one lucky S.O.B.

A lot of the guys in my class did pretty well, too. Bradford in Rochester, Hood in New York. Grady stayed in Syracuse and runs the University Medical Center. Foxworthy and Rothstein became partners and setup a radiology clinic outside Boston. Pies practices in L.A.; Dunston became an oral surgeon in Chicago. But some of my best and closest friends had it rough. Moore died early, heart attack. Zim got liver cancer and Billy drank himself to death. I wonder every once in a while how I'll go out, even though lying here, listening to train whistles and the light breathing of my sleeping lover, it all seems pretty abstract. I get asked about death and dying all the time. Oh, I see it, hear about it, talk about it, witness it, verify it, pronounce its certainty, and try to forget about it. I really don't have anything profound or otherwise to offer. The clock runs out on you; time's up. It helps a lot to believe in God, to have faith that all is ordained, but we've turned some corners in this country, come to believe in treatments and cures, gone from faith in snake oil to confidence in chemistry, trust in radiation. Whether I like it or not, my bedside manner doesn't hold a candle to penicillin. I don't discuss these thoughts, missing my friends, feeling nostalgia when train whistles blow west of town, being thankful for everything, yet missing everything, too.

I came to town looking for the job I saw advertised in the Post Standard, very fine print, Assistant GP wanted. At a hundred dollars a week it was more than I could hope for, and the doctor I worked for quickly became my mentor and friend. He had his office in a big white Victorian on the west hill of town, and from my rented room at Doyle's I could walk to the first-floor office of the house in under ten minutes. Most days, I went in early and came home late. It took a few weeks, but I got used to the trains on the New York Central and, within a few miles of each other toward the south, the Lehigh Valley, the Delaware and Lackawanna, and even farther south, the Erie. They made a symphony of night music, keeping time across the sleeping countryside.

One of my first patients turned out to be a railroad engineer. Marty was his name, made the night run to Albany from Niagara Falls. He always got delayed in the Buffalo switching yards, and by the time his train hit town, it was usually about 1 a.m. He'd be pushing the throttle to the speed limit. Two long and three short blasts on his horn signaled his wife, who listened for him south of the viaduct in their big farmhouse. I listened to his stories of railroading while checking his feet for what he said were shocks and tingles that "lit up" his toes. It's hard to tell what's wrong with a guy's feet by looking at them unless the problem's obvious. Marty's feet showed no signs of trouble. In fact, he had the healthiest feet I'd ever seen on a man over fifty, and I told him so.

"Well, Doc, they hurt just the same. I'm not making it up," he said.

Marty slipped back into his socks and shoes. As he headed out through the hallway to the waiting room, I told him to take it easy on the whistle and to try unlacing his shoes when he was sitting for long periods of time. He laughed with a certain knowing glint in his eyes. I never saw Marty in my office again.

Millie is another story. A bonafide hypochondriac and a marvelous baker of pies. She got my number pretty fast. She made me a fresh baked apple or berry pie at the rate of one per week. I loved a piece for breakfast with coffee, and I got into the habit of a slice at night, too. Before long, I put on eight or ten pounds and I was just keeping even with the pies. Delicious, but deadly. One night, Millie came in with one of her usual, unusual complaints, which I happened to have an ointment for, and in her wicker carrying basket she carried a tray of hot-cross buns. Well, that was it. I reached in, took one big bite and nearly went directly to heaven. How she knew they were my favorite from childhood, I'll never know, but I told her right away, and in no uncertain terms, that if she brought me one more irresistible thing to eat, I'd refuse to treat her. I'm still laughing at the memory of the look on Millie's face. She didn't know how to take it, and finally, she gave me that closed-eyes grin she was famous for. "Okay, Doc," she said, "I get it."

There's a dream I have every so often of old Doc Johnson rescuing fish from a series of ponds. He's watching himself, which is how I know it's a dream, from the rail of a bridge over the Oatka Creek where it flows through LeRoy. The ponds are different sizes. Big ones like lakes. Small ones like puddles. He's shouting from the bridge and pointing. Down below, his likeness is dashing from pond to pond, carrying fish. They're squirming, slippery. He drops a couple, too many to carry, but he keeps at it, carrying fish from smaller ponds to bigger ponds, and bigger ponds to smaller. From the bridge, where Doc Johnson and I seem to be the same figure, the fish appear to be about the same size and species, but Doc Johnson pays special attention to them up close and finally gets them all where he wants them to go. While he sits on a rock to rest, Doc Johnson (and I) walk back and forth, worrying about the day's work. Are the fish in the right ponds? Doc Johnson yells at the Doc Johnson look-alike to check the fish, check the ponds! I always wake up then. I don't like to have that dream too often. It reminds me of what I do, helping people jump from pond to pond until they run out of water.

It's usually morning by the time the dream passes, so I swing out of bed, go into the bathroom, cup cold water onto my face, use the toilet, shave, shower, and get ready for the day.

I like assisting Doc Johnson's son, Doc Johnson Jr. He's the spitting image of his father. Even on a routine appendectomy, he's hyper-aware of all possibilities, a surgeon's surgeon, and he works methodically and a little faster than most. I spot a tiny bleeder at the periphery of the abdominal cavity and pinch it off. Johnson carefully accounts for all tools and utensils, then closes. As we scrub, he makes sure to compliment me on the bleeder. That's the kind of guy you want to work with. Anybody would have noticed, but Dave Johnson will mention it; his ego's under control.

We always had a yard full of chickens when I was a boy. It became my job at some point to go out there and choose the chicken best for the week's eating. Ma could make a whole week's worth of chicken dishes; most of them, I'd say, were concoctions of the soup variety. When things got tight, there weren't that many chickens to choose from and I'd grown fond of one old brown hen, especially, so she survived all the cuts. One Saturday afternoon, Ma sent me out to get a chicken, and the brown hen was the only one left; I got a sinking feeling that my duty would have to overcome my loyalties. My favorite hen scratched around, clucking and strutting like a chicken does. It took me a while to get up the nerve, but I knew I couldn't return to the kitchen empty handed.

The hen really didn't put up much of a fight. I was sort of hoping that she would give me a hard time, run all around the barn, fly into the woods down the back hill, but she let me scoop her up in my arms, and as I wrung her neck, she clawed my forearm. At least she showed some fight at the end.

We had a dog named Douglas. Big, black. He could have been part Lab, but I don't remember if we ever knew. He was just Douglas to us, and as friendly and loyal as a dog could be. He liked to push his way between my mother's legs from behind, and sometimes he'd make her lose her balance. One time, the postman came to the door with a package, and as my mother opened the door, Douglas burst between her legs, knocking her forward and right out the door. The postman was completely taken by surprise; he was holding a fairly large package in both hands, getting ready to hand it to Ma. She pitched into him, grabbing for all she was worth for balance, they staggered back across the porch, and that's when Douglas charged to save her from the postman. The dog knocked them both flat and straddled the poor postman until my father heard the commotion and dashed out to the porch to pull Douglas back inside.

Don't ask me what was in the package. But I know that was the last time the post office sent any delivery to our place without calling first to make sure Douglas was locked up somewhere.

The Depression crept up on us. My father had worked his dried-apple business into a going concern, and he was on the verge of signing a contract with a company in Germany. He was selling real estate and insurance too, and I guess he expected to keep working at it, doing a little better all the time. That was the idea. Instead, everything he owned slipped away until one day the phone rang; it was the phone company. A voice told my father that if he didn't pay his bill, the phone would be taken out. "You can come get it," Pa said, "I'm not using it, anyway."

It was the last he heard from the phone company, but Ma was making arrangements of her own. She knew what little business Dad had a chance of doing depended on the telephone, so she made a deal. Dad, my brother and I would dig telephone pole holes in return for the monthly telephone charges. No money would change hands, just shovels.

It was hard work. Dad took us out along the county route where they were stringing wire, and we dug holes. We packed our own shovels, picks and post-hole diggers. We worked Monday, Tuesday and Wednesday. Then another family took the next three days. Nobody worked on the Sabbath. A photographer showed up one day and took a series of pictures of us digging holes, but I don't know what happened to the pictures. He said they'd be in the Canandaigua paper, but I never saw them.

I used to make it home from medical school whenever I could. It would most likely be late Saturday night if I wasn't pulling the early Sunday orderly shifts at Crouse Hospital. Those were rare weekends, but there were a few, and during my third year was when my brother started with the MS. At first, we were sure it was something else, temporary, treatable. He went to Florida to try the warm weather. He even tried a teaching job for a few months, but the symptoms kept advancing, and he came home. After a while we had to carry him places. He loved the night life and when he couldn't go out dancing any longer, his spirits really sank. Our favorite cousin, Isabel, visited from Buffalo, taking the train. She cried when she was alone with me, I'd cry too. We sat in the car at the train station in Clifton Springs and watched people amble in and out of the building, waiting on the platform for loved ones to arrive, and we'd think about Jordie, knowing soon he wouldn't be with us for jazz and dancing.

Jordie stayed in the upstairs bedroom at the front corner of the house, and his light would be on all night. I never got home before dark, so that glow in the upstairs window was a welcome sight. My brother was really my closest companion. He was just real good company. The night I came home to his dark window was the lowest night of my life. I don't know how long it took me to go inside, and if I remember those days that followed, I don't have much to say about them. It was agony, being a doctor and being helpless to do anything to save him. He didn't catch a single remission, either.

But I can't allow myself to dwell on it. In fact, I really don't think about not being able to help my brother, except I know, and he knew, I did what I could. I loved him, and all that does and doesn't mean. I suffered with him but not for him, and we both knew I'd do that too, for him, if I could. I guess we each get to do it for ourselves when the time comes. You could say God gives us loads we can carry, so maybe He's given me this life of helping other people with their suffering. I don't take it lightly, and I can't take it to the point of overdoing it. You can't help anybody else if you can't help yourself. I'd known for a long time that the night would come when my brother's window would be dark, but I've kept his light on inside me all these years since.

The sun isn't up yet, but it's announcing the day with pale light. Driving east into Batavia, I get a few minutes to plan the day. I can make rounds at Genesee between seven and eight, head over to St. Jerome's and check on my new admits and be back to Genesee for the 9:30 staff meeting. I'm hoping the ideas and preliminary plans for emergency room service make some more progress. I understand why some doctors don't want to get started down that road: loss of independence, loss of money, can't control patient load. But you can't stop change. There are too many people, not enough doctors, sickness and accidents don't happen on a schedule of doctors' office hours. When you need help, you need help, and that's what we're here for, to help people who need us. I concentrate on the Hippocratic Oath for a minute. It reinforces my sense of duty, not that I need it, but it doesn't hurt to remind myself. That damned phrase do no harm resonates a little too succinctly, and I let my mind wander, a series of old farm houses pass by the car on the right. I've admired one of them for years, its front porch recessed into the bulk of the building, squared columns molded into the framing like trim. It's a style fairly common around here, and I like the way it protects the front door from the weather while it still makes a welcoming appearance.

It's inside you, that security thing. My wife says I have the look. I notice my kids get comfortable when I'm around and always act disappointed when I have to leave them, which is often. I'll be sitting in the living room reading the paper, not paying much attention at all to them, but as soon as the phone rings and I jump up to get it, they ask me where I'm going, even though they heard the phone ring, too. For me, it's a luxury to walk into the office from my home. It means less wasted time driving back and forth from home to office and more time being around my family. I'm not actually with them most of the time, but I can feel them near, hear the thumping of footsteps upstairs, and pick up occasional tones of their voices through the walls. Just being close like that gives me a lot of confidence and peace. I'm working for all of us, not just me, or the patient. Surrounded by that sense of love and support I think makes me a better doctor. At least, I hope so; I'd hate to be kidding myself.

Most of my patients require medicine, prescribed doses of pharmaceuticals to treat ailments, fight their diseases. I prescribe all kinds of things and patients often tuck the scripts into a pocket or purse and promptly forget all about getting them filled. Some patients get the scripts filled and never take the medicine. That's one good reason to make house calls.

Ned is a good case in point. He's got blood pressure problems like a lot of overweight, part-time farmers around here. He believes that hauling hay and chasing a few cows will offset the loads of meat and potatoes his wife spreads on the dinner table every night. On my last house call over there, I asked to use the bathroom. It's off the kitchen, close to the sitting room where Ned and his wife Julia spend a good deal of time by the wood stove, watching TV. I'm in the bathroom, washing my hands, and while the water's running, I open the medicine cabinet over the sink. Half the lower shelf is lined with opaque, orange bottles from the drug store. Blood pressure pills. A row of plastic bottles full of pills. Looks like Ned picks up prescriptions and stashes them. A lot of good they're doing in the medicine cabinet. When I return to the kitchen table and sit across from Ned, I ask him about his intake schedule.

"Oh, I'm supposed to take them three times a day, Doc." He grins with all the enthusiasm of a lifer. "Morning, noon and night."

What can I say? This is where the patient is responsible for his own treatment. For whatever reason, Ned wants to believe that spending the time and money on the prescriptions is actually as good as taking the medicine, and he knows what he's supposed to do. The line-up of full pill bottles tells me I have to try something to get him to take his medicine, but without offending him, talking down to him.

"Since you're doing so well," I say, "maybe we can dispense with the blood pressure pills for a few weeks and see what happens."

He gives me a twisted, quizzical look.

"Unless you think you need to keep taking them."

"Well, Doc," and then he told me the whole story about going to the drug store, getting the prescriptions filled, bringing them home to the downstairs bathroom where he could take them at meal times, and then how he forgot all about taking the pills. He said he felt better knowing the pills were there if he really needed them, but he didn't like the idea of taking pills every day. It made no sense to me, but Ned was so sincere, and so embarrassed, that I had to laugh and tell him it was all right to stock up, and that taking a few pills every day couldn't hurt. He promised not to ignore my advice again, actually apologized for not following doctor's orders. I'll stop by again in a few days to see how he's doing.

*   *   *   *   *

We were riding bikes to Darien Center and back. Cool, low sun, early Sunday afternoon, Marj, two of her brothers and me. I could tell they were holding back a little for me, my hard pedaling days clearly behind me. Racing bicycles held no attraction, and a leisurely jaunt over the gentle hills of Allegheny Road was plenty of exercise for me. Besides, I was getting lost in the sight of Marj pumping away in her tight riding trousers. The easy flow of cornfields and farm houses along the way enhanced my light-headed mood.

We figured if our timing was good we could return in time to watch the Silver Bullet Special pass on its way from New York City to Buffalo. By all predictions the train would break the speed record for the 400-mile route and make big news for the New York Central Railroad. We caught the train, all right. It was making well over 100 miles an hour, and we lined up its approach from the overpass, sighting the pin prick of headlight on the eastern horizon of the track, and, whoosh, before we knew it, the big steam engine and its train of silver cars flew under us and vanished. I felt like a witness to history, and to everyone's surprise, I out-pedaled them home.

When we burst into Marj's house, her mother turned from where she hunkered near the radio and gave us the hush sign with her finger to her lips. Through the static on the radio console, the words of President Roosevelt: a sneak attack on Pearl Harbor. All at once the Silver Bullet was old news and nearly a lost memory. The world changed in that one afternoon while we were out riding bicycles. All able-bodied men dashed off to the draft board.

That's the day I fell in love, and I've been in love with the same woman ever since.

Standing alone at the kitchen sink, looking out at the morning, I wondered how I would tell Danny about his friend's car accident. I heard him on the back stairs, coming down. I kept peeling the orange, separating the sections so as not to tear them into juicy pieces. I laid them on a saucer and turned toward the table.

Dan poured a cup of coffee and sat next to me. He wasn't fully awake but he smiled, anyway. Dan fingered an orange section and popped it into his mouth, making a mushing sound as he chewed.

I thought of the 3 a.m. ER call, the young man stretched out on the table, his muscled body unmarked, his brain swelling. His head injury was most likely beyond our capability of treatment, a situation calling for nature's best luck and lots of answered prayers.

Dan sipped at the rim of his coffee cup. "We had a record day yesterday, put up seven wagon loads. Worked past dark."

Dan's farm job really energized him, and his friendships with the boys who worked the hay fields and the barns' high mows had grown strong over the last two summers. Their crew criss-crossed the fields in a tandem of tractor, baler and wagon, and their tendency to push themselves to higher and higher standards of production fueled competition and strengthened the bonds between them. It was a rare conversation that didn't include a reference to the farm, or to Dan's close friend, Chuck. Dan loved the farm work, the camaraderie he found in the fields and the family solidarity gathered around the noonday table. The time for Danny to head out to work neared, and I dreaded my duty.

"Dan, I've got some bad news. About your friend." I don't recall the words; there wasn't much to say. I was in the same spot Chuck's father and mother were in, and now, Dan, too, and soon everyone else in town and the surrounding hamlets and county farms. Bound together in the common story of one of our young men fighting for his life in the hospital, his struggle, a painful reminder of how suddenly life turns from plans to prayers.

Dan left for the farm that day, the spring gone from his step. I suppose he didn't know what else to do, but I think he had to see if my story was true. Not that he doubted me, but he doubted that life could be so arbitrary, even cruel, to treat his friend like that.

When Dan left for college in September he took memories of the farm and his feelings with him. We talked about the accident a number of times during his breaks, and I could sense that his enthusiasm for the immediate satisfactions of physical labor had ebbed, replaced by what I would call an edgy existentialism. I wasn't pleased, but over time his fatalism gave way to renewed faith and exuberance, for poetry and literature as it turned out. He liked stories where love and loyalty endured tragedy and loss. I could see Dan's trust turning toward language and the expression of emotion impossible for him through any other means.

When my friends ask me how he is and what he's doing now, I say Danny's a poet, and their faces brighten in wonder and, I like to think, a little irony, too. I guess a lot of doctors want to be writers. I'll bet a lot of writers would like to be doctors, too.

So much of what I do, what I see, seems inexplicable by science alone. We refer to the practice of medicine as an art. Maybe for Dan the practice of art is a kind of medicine, and we're both working away at the same candle from either end. I doubt we'll make it to the middle, but the candle's burning shorter.

I've been practicing medicine a long time, yet just last night, it seems, Barney and I took off from the Good Shepherd to answer an ambulance call on North McBride Street. It's February, Syracuse, of course it's snowing, hard pack under a nice fresh coating of falling snow. We found the address, an old rooming house. We pull up to the snow bank along the curb, and we scramble inside to see what we can do. As it turns out, the first- floor tenant made the call, and she hadn't seen the guy who lived upstairs for two days, which alarmed her because they shared coffee every morning. We went up to the room with her. The door was unlocked; we found him in bed. He'd passed away in his sleep, dead maybe couple of days. After helping the woman back to her place — she was very unsteady on her feet, nearly collapsing on the stairs — we got the stretcher out of the ambulance and went back upstairs to the guy's room. That's when the fun started.

The guy must have weighed over two hundred and fifty pounds, and he wasn't going to help us get him to the hospital where we could transfer him to the morgue. Barney shot me his tell-tale, cross-eyed wince as we leaned over the bed. Well, it cracked me up. Barney didn't say a word. We got the body onto the stretcher, grabbed the handles and squeezed through the doorway and headed down the stairs. Barney farted all the way: Phfft, Phfft, Phfft. We both started laughing.

I hadn't noticed how icy the front steps were when we came in, and just when it looks like we'll make it to the ambulance, I slip. I try to catch my balance, put my hand out, the damned stretcher tilts and our body slides out into the snow. Jesus, there he is, sprawled on the steps. Barney slipped down too, so the two of us are sitting in the snow with this corpse between us, and Barney, acting embarrassed, apologizes to the guy for dropping him in the snow. Apologizing to a corpse! I laughed so hard my sides ached. Then, we got everything pulled together and drove back to the hospital. The best I can say about that is we never dropped a live patient, and that's quite a record considering some of the fixes we got ourselves into.

When you see all the lousy things that can happen to people, you wonder about God's will, whether God has anything to do with it. People always ask, why this, why that? I suppose the easiest answer is to say, it's God's will, but I find that pretty unsatisfying even if it's true. Since God isn't saying much about it; we doctors get to do the explaining. Most of the time, you determine cause of death, why that one particular cause was the cause of death is an educated guess many times, and that's where faith comes in. It helps some people to believe a loved one got called upstairs to serve in a higher capacity. It can be comforting. We humans need to believe in higher causes, especially when a youngster or a baby dies. It's a death out of order. We need to know the cause and the reason. Then, we set about to prevent the same thing happening to other youngsters, babies. We invest time and money into research, studies and trials, applying all kinds of techniques and theories. We're always searching for ways to discover causes and to treat symptoms and to find cures. When you get involved in all of that, it's hard not to believe something beyond you and science is working. Maybe the more passionate you are about fighting disease, the more you feel a part of that bigger thing.

The day my wife and younger daughter got into a car accident I was out of town, and I returned after the fact to find them both in the hospital. I asked all the usual questions of myself. What if I had been driving? What if that dog hadn't dashed into the road in front of the car? What if Marj hadn't swerved into the pole, but had run over the dog instead? I would likely have hit the dog, but that one time, maybe I'd have swerved, too. Was it simply fate, the car hitting the pole? And why didn't the impact kill one or both of them? For a second or two, it might be a sign to me not to get too full of myself in this business of helping people, as if I were immune to the same fates as my patients.

I've had the conversations without words you have in your head. Maybe that's how you communicate with God. I don't know for sure, but I do have faith that I'm not working alone in this world. I have purpose that transcends me, and over the course of my life, I've sometimes felt directed, although I'll always say, if asked, that I do what I do out of free will. The truth may be more complex.

* * * * *

My mother's good nature masked her determination to motivate her grade-school students to learn and to put their talents to good use. She was the same with her family. My aunts and uncles were accustomed to visiting on Sundays, talking up family sagas, politics, local affairs and events, what so-and-so said about such-and-such. Ma would listen for just so long before she started talking more and they began listening more. They ate her cookies and drank the lemonade Jordie and I never got during the week.

By dinner time, Ma solved everybody's problems — in theory, at least. All they had to do was return home and put her advice into practice. No one ever did, of course, and the following Sunday they would bring back the same old tales, and get the same old advice from Ma, but having grown up on the farm together, Ma and her brothers and sisters couldn't seem to get along without each other. Bea couldn't have children; Millie couldn't stop having them. Bennie was always complaining about machinery and old cars, and Bert wouldn't see a doctor about the sore on his shin. Ma enjoyed being the older sister, the leader of the flock.

As we grew older, the aunts and uncles visited less often. Everyone got bogged down, busy with things. Graduations, birthdays and Christmas still gathered everyone together, but the strains of growing families and the Depression took their toll. We were lucky to get one store-bought present under the tree. Ma baked for a solid week before the big days, making pies, cakes, cookies and taffy for each of her nine brothers and sisters and their families, while at the same time contributing enough chicken dinners to the Methodist church to feed a dozen out-of-work families. One year she fed a whole shift of nurse trainees at the Sanitarium. My brother and I thought Ma was normal.

Hospitals didn't pay so much, but there was always work. Sickness takes no holiday, as they say, and Ma could see that doctors, nurses, orderlies and all kinds of kitchen and janitorial help were in constant demand. At the top of the heap were the doctors. Somewhere along the line, my mother decided I would become a doctor. When I talk about free will, destiny and fate, I'm talking about my mother!

Ma was always a couple of steps ahead of the rest of us. She knew the Dean at Hobart by first name before I even applied. In fact, she had baked him an apple pie a week before I was accepted to start freshman year, it took me a while to find out she'd talked with him. I wonder how he maintained his judgment after one of her pies. At the same time, I'm glad she didn't get to my chemistry prof with a pot of her baked beans.

When my brother applied to college two years after me, he made sure to keep Ma away from the whole process. Even though it wasn't so complicated in those days, he faked ambitions to study out west, far away from the reach of fresh baked beans and apple pies. We laughed like hell about that since he ended up at Hobart with me. That story kept us laughing a few times while we were camped out over the post office in a cold water flat. The drive home for the Saturday night bath was full of happy expectation in those days. There was always plenty of food and hot water.

•　　•　　•　　•　　•

You try to avoid the politics of medicine, but it's all around, and in most cases, I know things about people, what they do and why they do it. On the confidentiality issue, I'm about as safe as a vault at the bank.

The abortion debate flares and smolders in predictable cycles around here like it does in most places. My female patients often want to know my position on it, and if I told them, no matter what I said, I'd be making enemies for no good reason. But I can say one thing: I didn't go through med school and two residencies to be an abortionist. I know where to send pregnant women if need be.

Abortion is one of those issues that brings out the worst in people on all sides. And, I've got to tell you, I sympathize with the doctor who performs abortions and risks his life for it. No amount of demagoguery or demonstrating is going to put a stop to copulating. If you can't stop that part of nature, you can't stop people from wanting to change the consequences, either. The law is great until you find out it doesn't agree with you. My conscience won't let me do abortions, but my conscience also won't let me act against those who do.

We get an adoption case every so often, and most of them work out better when you involve as few people as possible. One woman is going to deliver a baby and doesn't want to; another woman wants a baby and can't deliver a baby for some reason, ever. If I get a chance to help out in a situation like that, I will.

I've never seen, and I've never heard of, female-only conception. The old local adage is that every time a girl gets pregnant, a guy leaves town. That's our small-town version of population control!

Until recently, the guy was persona non gratis, the culprit who wasn't the one ballooning up, pushing the carriage, nursing and fussing like a mother hen. But we still have a couple of buffoons running around town bragging about their dastardly deeds. Lately, I think the whole thing has gotten both more serious and more casual. The stigma about premarital sex is pretty well shot, but getting pregnant, that's still not a good deal. The guy is not so likely to leave town, now, and he may not be so quick to marry the girl either, but there's an acceptance in the community that these things happen and the stigma that often drove the guy out of town is gone. Now, a new father has status even if he's not married. He can stick around, keep his head up, take turns with the diapers and have a chance to amount to something. You know, you can fool around and fall in love, as the song goes.

I wish I could say that about everybody, about how the world is going. If I didn't read the papers, watch TV, open my eyes to what goes on, I'd be more hopeful. Not that I'm not hopeful, you can't give up hope, but some people among us don't care about anything or anyone except themselves at this very minute. They make it tough for the rest of us.

I guess if you don't like the way things are, you can vote against them. You just have to understand that you only get one vote, and if you aren't satisfied with that, you can get involved, organize, write letters or whatever. You've got every right, including the right to complain. I voted against FDR four times. I would again, but I still had to get up every morning and do what I had to do, no matter who was president. At least I always believe I'm voting for the United States of America.

As flawed, confusing, and competitive as it is, the place is alive and free for most of us. A lot of poor people have gotten rich here, and there's always somebody who makes more money than you do; that's the meaning of rich!

Just yesterday, a guy told me I was rich because I was a doctor, and I told him I was rich, all right, but not because I'm a doctor. I'm rich in spite of being a doctor. Well, he walked away scratching his head. I started laughing on the way home in my car, and I'm still laughing. He had no idea what I was talking about.

* * * * *

Mother comes to mind often. Nothing mysterious about what she was thinking; her thoughts and observations were hooked up to her mouth.

My father, on the other hand, said very little and he said it often. I have clear memories of Dad sitting at his desk in the downstairs hallway. He pinned a calendar to the wall there, and the phone sat on the back corner where he could pick up the receiver in one motion. The stack of unpaid bills was neatly set on the blotter pad in the center. The drawers on the left side were stuffed full of personal letters; on the right, the drawers were empty. I didn't really take much notice at the time, but looking back, I see the pile of unpaid bills growing higher, and I see Dad making check marks on the calendar and then just staring at them. Like I said, since I was always on my way out the door, chasing my boy's life, I never hung around my father. He was very serious and honest; he wasn't exactly what you'd call fun.

One time, he sent Jordie and me out to clean the ice house, but when he came out to see how we were doing, you could see he wasn't happy. "A boy does a boy's job, but two boys do no job at all." I still remember him saying that. Did he laugh then, or raise his hands in frustration? Not Dad. He just turned and went back inside the house. The old man we called him.

But thinking about him, how little he said, I wonder if Ma didn't actually do the talking for him. She certainly knew how he felt about things. Why not, she seemed to know what everyone else was thinking before they said it. And he had a funny kind of gentleness about him that made them a good pair. It was as if Ma kept him just calm enough to weather his disappointments. You know, he went from a businessman on the verge of making it big to a guy selling apples from the back of a Model A truck.

I tried to go with him one Saturday morning, and he gave me the meanest look he could muster. "Go back inside and study, Benjamin. You aren't growing up in my house to become a peddler."

He could have whacked me with a Louisville Slugger. I went up to my room and took out the dictionary to look up the definition of "peddler." I didn't like what I found in the diction- ary, but it struck me that Dad now saw himself as a peddler and that really distressed me. I went back outside and stood in the empty driveway. Everything was quiet, no cars going by, no dogs barking, and no one in sight. I thought of my father thinking of himself as a peddler; it took me awhile to stop cry- ing, and when I did, I walked back inside, went up to my room, flopped on the bed and opened Gibbons' book on the rise and fall of the Roman Empire. I kept at it until supper time.

I haven't changed my routine much from that day. I read whenever I'm not seeing patients or driving to and from some- where. On vacation I read in bed until midnight as if it's the grandest luxury in the world, which it is to me.

Danny got me out in the canoe last summer, sharpie that he is, he took the stern seat and that put my back to him as well as made me do the hard paddling. We were well out into the middle of the lake when he asked me to tell him about my father. I didn't know what to say, of course, but I said I'd never been out in a canoe with my old man, not once; and my father never told me anything I can remember about his father.

•   •   •   •   •

Marj came into the bedroom tonight wrapped in an afghan bath robe, and when she climbed into bed to read her book, I couldn't help but remember her naked, not so long ago it seems, standing in that same doorway, smiling at me as I lay under a sheet and light blanket. It was late May, Marj had done the dishes, and the kids were all asleep in their beds. She switched off the light, and as my eyes adjusted, her silhouette backed by the moon angling through the window came close, and then she covered me. How we made love that night warms me these umpteen years later, while my lover lies fast asleep beside me. I hope love-making scenes play in her dreams, too.

COUSIN HENRY

My father said that my grandmother lived in dreamland. I didn't know what he meant by that, or why he laughed when he said it. All I knew was that Gram told great stories. If they didn't focus on a runaway horse, a train wreck or a fire that ripped through brick walls and lay waste to half a city, the stories were about family escapades, with some kind of dramatic climax. The characters she told about never failed to get my attention. She was a walking, talking chronicle of the events and people in her life, and I, for one, couldn't get enough.

Cousin Henry whistled Broadway tunes. He outdanced and outsang all the men folk in the county; he was a flamboyant dresser in a county of farmers and shop-keepers. His tweed vests, linen-lined slacks and patent-leather spats made him the "dandy" other men wanted their gals to steer clear of. Although he didn't see so well, he sported a collection of glasses ranging from dark horned rims to a monocle that trailed a red ribbon down his left cheek. The glasses distinguished him from the run-of-the-mill Batavian. Gram said you could see him coming a block up the street.

Cousin Henry treated his cousin Mary the way a lady liked to be treated, is what I figured. In all the stories I ever heard that included Cousin Henry, he was the beneficiary of Gram's admiration and respect. His deeds never indebted him, and his investments never seemed to sour. His time was not frittered away on nonsense like most other men's. Gram made Henry sound like a modern-day Ben Franklin.

Of course, none of us kids had been alive in the times Gram depicted with such flair. We hadn't run down the farm house steps to drool over Cousin Henry's Packard coupe, but we whiffed the luscious scent from the upholstery in Gram's words, and we pictured Cousin Henry waving farewell from the main platform of the Jackson Street train station, while the engine churned up a full head of steam before disappearing into the rain clouds toward New York City.

Gram missed Cousin Henry, but every once in a while a letter would turn up and Gram would study it closely before reading it to us directly from the creased pages. It was exciting hearing Gram read. Cousin Henry captivated us with descriptions of his travels. He "hobnobbed" with Vice President Wallace at a summer festival on the Potomac. He sailed across Chesapeake Bay in a gale; he sold cars to rich people in Norfolk. The bank president wore spats just like Cousin Henry's.

Gram said he'd moved farther south and was acting in musical plays near Savannah. He moved to Mobile, then to Miami. For a long time, she didn't hear from Cousin Henry. One day, Gram told my mother she'd received a note from him. "He's assumed a darker tone," she said, and soon enough, stories about Cousin Henry took on a darker tone, too. Recollections of the brilliant boy in school were tempered by parenthetical phrases about Cousin Henry's "wayward tendencies," somehow, he never quite "fit in." Cousin Henry's "eye for the wrong kind of girls" required the getaway speed of his Packard coupe more than once.

Those letters from Cousin Henry raised doubts and sadness in Gram's voice. She had clearly enjoyed her cousin more than anything; they had been young together. When her worries got the best of her, Gram began asking my mother if it wouldn't be a good idea to visit Cousin Henry on the family's spring trip to Fort Myers Beach. Mom explained why we couldn't do that in the short period of time we had for vacation. Cousin Henry's place would probably be far out of the way.

A year later, my father and mother decided we'd drive to Fort Myers Beach again for a vacation. The plan was not to be discussed with anyone, lest friends, relatives and (mainly) patients would line up for office visits, as if we were going away forever. My sisters and I kept the secret until the latest Cousin Henry letter arrived, right before Christmas. "Maybe we can stop at Cousin Henry's on the way," I whispered to Mom, loud enough so Gram could overhear. Later that evening my mother and father announced we would take Gram—my mother's mother Mary—on the Florida trip.

●　　●　　●　　●　　●

By the time we reached Jacksonville, my sisters had eaten half the box of Schrafts chocolates and Gram the other half. A couple of nugets had slipped from "somebody's" lap and worked their way into the seat, "mussing" the upholstery, my mom said. The whole back seat and carriage area of the station wagon was a sticky mess, but as Gram must have said fifty times since we left, "There's no place like home; that's why we always take it with us."

Mom scolded us kids for the back seat rat's nest, but her tone was clearly aimed at Gram. Dad smiled to himself and settled deep into the driver's seat. Gram sat erect, eyes set on the back of Mom's head. If you listened closely, you could hear Gram whistling softly through her teeth.

When we hit Daytona, Dad drove straight onto the beach. Waves broke way off shore and ran in right under the car tires. Dad gave it the gas and we roared along beside two motorcycles until Mom yelled he was "setting a bad example." He backed off and cruised to a stop on the flat, hard sand. We all jumped out; it was pretty exciting. Gram took off her shoes and let the water wash over her feet, while Mom and Dad waded around closer to the car.

Florida is a very long state. From the back seat, it looks like an endless tunnel of jungle. Shades of green wall you in, squeeze the road, hover overhead. Orange juice shacks play hide and seek with the sun. Blistered pick-ups pull out from unmarked hideaways, and even Dad drove with caution. Some of the drivers looked younger than me, and I was a good two years short of my New York driver's license. Florida is light and heavy at the same time. Maybe it was the hot sun. I wondered if it slowed some things down, like walking and talking, and speeded other things up, like living and dying.

Inside the car, we all succumbed to the heat of the day. My father just kept driving, following the simple directions taped to the rear view mirror: Route 1, all the way to a turn onto State 209 to County 19 to Louisa Lake Road, 2106. After the third or fourth turn, the roads dwindled to trails and then became paths. We backed up and turned around a couple of times. Our Chevy wagon seemed to get bigger and wider, as low palm fronds and wild, thorny Bougainvillea slapped through the open car windows.

When we hit the clearing, Dad cranked the wheel hard to the left to avoid a huge brindle dog lying in the middle of the lane. The dog lay still as stone. We stopped. Dad got out first and stretched his bare arms over his head. "Grand Central Station! All out!"

Mom stayed put. Barbara Ann and I scrambled out, not waking Melanie, fast asleep in a pile of pillows. Gram followed, slow to get her feet under her. We stood transfixed for a moment in the saucer of clearing where six trimmed citrus trees and a couple of shacks made a kind of "outback" farm. On the far side of the clearing, what looked like a cigar store Indian, sitting bare-chested on a rough-hewn bench, raised his hand. Cousin Henry. Gram waved but stayed near the car, ready to lean against it.

One of the shacks had a back door, and I ran to it with my sister close behind. The shack was bent like an arm with a cubby for the dog at the elbow. A chest-high plank butted against a zinc sink draining to a hole in the floor. A big old knife lay next to a split melon, and Barbara Ann reached for it reflexively. "You could chop a tree with this thing!"

On the far side of the clearing, Dad made conversation with Cousin Henry. The old man didn't appear to have much to say, but I'm sure Dad got a lot out of it. By the time Gram made it to the bench, Barbara Ann and I had found the ropey-haired Negro woman in the one-room shack at the edge of the clearing behind Cousin Henry's digs. I guess she was young compared to him, but she looked old to us. We couldn't understand a word she said, but she smiled when she offered us a sip of some dark juice from a glass jar.

We headed back toward the car. Melanie sat up and looked around to make sure we were all there, then curled immediately back into sleep. Mom got in and sat sideways in the front seat with the door open. We knew what she thought about the whole scene by the look on her face. Barbara Ann started to say something stupid, but I pulled her away from the car, and she chased me around the yard until we both fell down, giggling.

But Gram remained with Cousin Henry. They sat side-by-side on the bench, both staring out at the humble clearing he must have been describing in his letters, letters she'd read to us during story times. He wrote that it was a "paradise on earth," a "blessing from God for hard roads traveled," and "my little corner of Heaven."

They looked like figurines propped under a fichus tree in a museum diorama. Cousin Henry, shirtless, his tanned skin stretched taut between narrow shoulders; Gram, stick-skinny, house dress fluttering about her knees, her rimless glasses flashing like pooled rain under the afternoon sun.

After Cousin Henry told Gram he'd take a "rain check" on her offer of "supper someplace nice," it was time to leave. We all piled into the Chevy. Dad steered the car back along the way we'd come, careful to avoid the larger overhanging limbs, accelerating gradually as we cleared the narrower lanes and pulled out onto the paved road. A good half hour passed before we hit the cross-state highway that would take us toward Fort Myers. Heavy, hot air blasted through the windows. Gram pulled herself forward over the back of the front seat.

"How did Henry look to you, Ben?"

I look back at that scene under the fichus tree and see an old photograph, the kind my great-grandmother Ada used to arrange in her studio. Henry sits, straight-backed and affable. Gram leans slightly toward the hole of his mouth. It looks like they belong on the slab of bench under that tree forever. What an eventful life he's had, he might be telling her, and how happy he is that she's finally caught up with him to hear the latest installments in person. And, what is she thinking... that this coat-hanger of a man can't possibly be my Cousin Henry... I can't possibly be his Cousin Mary who, after all these years, must now reunite with him to learn there's nothing left for either of us but to talk of the past?

Not long after that trip, Gram tumbled backward from the piano stool in our music room. Dad checked her over and sent her to a couple of specialists who found nothing to worry about, but he scheduled her for a series of tests at Roswell Park clinic as a precaution. The Roswell Park doctors discovered the cancer on her first visit. Gram took the news stoically. Her morning walks continued but shortened gradually until she struggled to go beyond her driveway. She doubled up on Dad's Manhattans when she came over, which was often. "If one is good, two is better," she liked to say.

I was away at college when Mom's call drew me quickly home to sit beside Gram's death bed. Gram asked me to tell her some stories about college, and I did the best I could. What I will remember about Gram, as long as I am able, is the way she could dramatize people's everyday lives, channeling their hopes and fears.

The family was working on a Presbyterian Mission in the Arizona desert one summer, and our only contact with home, far to the east, was through Gram's weekly letters. I remember most of the "news" from home as being rather mundane and not all that compelling, but the subtext of the letters played on our collective guilt about how we'd left her all alone for the summer. Just when her last letter seemed to auger into church supper talk, Gram applied the quill.

"Did you hear about the fire?"

If not for that hook, we might have stayed longer in Arizona.

FETCHING THE DOG

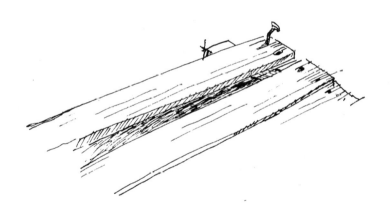

I pulled into the driveway in front of a little country ranch house over near South Alabama, just after dark. It was late April, chilly. Bob and Ray were standing near their parked cars, and they welcomed me with great amusement.

"What are you guys doing here?"

I couldn't have been more surprised. My closest friends, doctors from neighboring towns, and me, all standing outside the same country farm house on a dark spring evening at the same time.

"Looks like we all got the call," Ray said. "I say we draw straws."

Bob's chuckle masked his annoyance but not by much. "Six a.m. scrub for me. You two can wangle it out, g'night!" Bob headed for his car.

Ray sighed, "I guess I better go in with you." And, he did.

The front porch door opened directly onto the living room where a bedraggled woman sat sideways on a sway-back davenport. "'Bout time you made a house call, Dr. Ray. I call you five times and you come once. Not good odds— and who are you?" She looked at me with her rheumy, mad eyes. "I never called you, whatever the name. You a doctor too, I s'pose."

I looked at Ray and he looked at me and we both started laughing.

The woman got so upset with us that she got into a coughing jag, and we had to quit laughing. "You're a son-of-a-bitch, Dr. Ray, I wouldn't let you look up my ass with somebody else's eye-ball!"

That really got us laughing, and Ray slapped me on the shoulder as he backed away for the door. "She's all yours, doctor." I heard relief in his laugh.

And then I was standing in front of her. Alone. I quickly slipped into my doctor mode and observed the patient. "That's a nasty-looking gash on your leg, Missus…"

"Fripp. It hurts like hell, but it ain't bleed'n like it was."

I knelt to get a closer look. The cut was long but not deep, more like a gouge. Although it was unlikely, I thought about Tetanus. "We'll have to clean it up. Maybe put on gauze and tape to pull it together. How'd you do this, anyway, Mrs. Fripp?"

"Fetching the dog."

Mrs. Fripp had gone out to the back stoop to call the dog and managed to catch her foot and fall down the steps. The dog still wouldn't come to her, and she'd crawled back up the steps and into the kitchen where she placed a few calls to whoever she could think of to help her. She was pretty vague about names and numbers, but she had obviously reached a number of doctors.

I unlatched my bag, fished out a roll of gauze, laid out the adhesive and a pair of scissors. I sponged the wound with peroxide and washed the entire lower leg with warm soap and water before I wrapped and taped.

"That'll do you for now," I said. "If you can get your husband to drive you over to my office tomorrow, I'll give it the first-class treatment." That's when she asked me to get the dog in for her. "Her name is Georgie."

The kitchen light was on, which made it really black outside the back door window. While I was looking for a wall switch for the back porch light, I spotted the hammer lying among a batch of tools on the countertop. I picked it up and opened the door. A bare light bulb stuck out of a socket next to the back door frame. I pulled the chain. Suddenly, it made sense, how Mrs. Fripp fell. The stoop consisted of four planks lying across parallel runners of cement blocks. A couple of crude planks led down to the yard. One long rusty nail angled out between the top step and the side rail. Even in that weak light, the nail head glistened with dried blood. I took the hammer to the nail just as the tiniest dog I've ever seen scampered up the steps and through the open door behind me. The joyous cries of "Georgie! Georgie! Georgie!" still make me smile when I think of that night.

I finished with the nail and went back into Mrs. Fripp's living room. Georgie nuzzled her neck, wagging that little rag tail like sixty. "Guess you're my doctor now," Mrs. Fripp said, not unhappily.

"That's good, Mrs. Fripp, but I've got one strict rule: only one house call per patient per night under normal circumstances, and I determine the circumstances."

"Understood, doctor."

I think I caught her smiling. I winked and was halfway to the car before I realized I hadn't charged her, but I kept walking, got in and backed out into the road. Headed for home, the headlights plugging away at the dark, I thought how small that dog was and how big was the joy of Mrs. Fripp. That was worth all the tea in China.

A LIFE OF THE MIND

It never occurs to you after a lifetime of knowing you're going to die that it might actually happen. It comes as a huge surprise to everyone who knows you, but let me tell you from first hand experience, no one is more surprised than yours truly. Imagine all the things you have lying around that you wouldn't want anyone, including your nearest and dearest, to get into. Stuff that needs a lot of explaining ... People draw their own conclusions about your business, and quickly, so it's a good thing to have the chance to explain the whys, hows, wherefores and what-ifs. I thought I'd lived a life of no regrets, but the last thing flashing through my shell-shocked mind on the pitch down the cellar stairs was that goddamned folder in my bottom desk drawer at school.

I couldn't muster the courage to destroy it when I should have, and then, well, I guess I pretty much put it on hold. What would you do with your once in a lifetime love letters, the ones from your secret, illicit and dangerous affair with the dream girl right off the cover of Vogue? Yeah, I know, you would have burned the evidence already, chalked the whole thing up to experience—that is, if you'd been crazy enough to get involved in the first place.

Oh, that night in her parents' living room, when they were supposed to be in Buffalo for a concert or a play, I don't remember which, and they came home early, headlights sweeping the back wall of the room through the big picture window, right above the couch where she and I snuggled in juicy bliss. Delight flashing to panic, the door opening in the kitchen stairwell, the sticky front door lock, the howling dog, the belly flop onto the lawn, no shots fired, no cops called, no phones ringing where my wife dozes in front of the TV.

Imagine, soaked and muddy from the tumble across the night lawn, toweling off in my dank garage, groping for the light switch, still charged up, hard as a frightened banana.

You wouldn't want someone to get into those letters from a girl like that, would you? Her words in that loopy calligraphy tweaked the hairs of my crotch. Images of us rolling into the back seat, me looking into her world and she into mine, and that other world going into orbit between us...never mind. If I described it for you, the kaleidoscopes, the waterfalls, the angels singing, you'd laugh at me.

So here's what happens so fast after you leave the scene that it makes your head spin like a freaked-out top. The principal calls in a colleague to sort through your desk. The town organizes a memorial service. Your wife buys a new dress for the first time since her wedding. Your friends speak at the memorial, Doctor Childress appoints Kevin to take your place as Dean of Students, and your wife throws up three Manhattans on her new dress, not necessarily in that order, but that's how it looks from here and I'm already jumping ahead in the story.

Many years ago, I fell in love with teaching school. I say this not to justify myself, but to put into words the feelings of purpose and joy the whole business set in motion for me. When you love what you study, you surround yourself with the trappings of your love, like wall posters. My all-time favorite, numeral 2s in a blue sky of 5s, free as bumblebees, fascinated any number of students over the years, and the poster served as a spark to conversation, then connection. A teacher who taped mod posters on his wall must be okay, right? I got very comfortable with the way the energy of youth parades through your life. You hear your name sung over and over, teacher, teacher. There's something seductive about it. You have status; you feel good about things. People say you're smart; you like to think so. Your bottom drawer collects notes of thanks, tribute and affection.

How many times do you think Socrates fell off his log, anyway?

What did all we esteemed faculty talk about in the corridors of our prime?

Lunch duty, the quarterback's sister, the one-armed shop teacher, library rats, school bus routes, fat conditioning coaches, or Harvard's curriculum standards, when things got really boring. Then, the girl walks into the smoky faculty lounge seeking permission for field experience credit. Everybody looks at me, because I'm the Dean. I tell her she can have field experience credit for anything her little heart desires, but first, I have to review a formal proposal, later. The delightful (and gorgeous) student parts the cigarette smoke as I hold the door open for her. Dean-like, I assume the pose of the ethical gentleman. The French Lit teacher smirks at me.

The welt on her upper arm was a perfect imperfection burned into her by an errant hawser on a ski tow when she was a child. I can't say how my attention got drawn to that imperfection on an otherwise too-perfect physique, taut olive skin and all, but my lips longed to pucker on that Blarney Stone of a skin bubble, and that longing turned into an obsession, and for too long that obsession blocked all rationality from my thinking. While I was extremely careful not to look like I felt – whacked out in love with a girl half my age – I did worry about what a few people might think of my indiscretions if they happened to discover them to be factually true. I couldn't stand to be thought of as an ordinary philanderer, but what other kind is there?

I get a lot of reading time, here. I've gotten interested in Cleopatra, who stole the hearts of strapping men and wreaked havoc on orderly societies, while leaving no single, accurate physical description that survives to this day. I truly believe that Cleopatra is an archetype that can pop up anytime, anywhere. Like in a high school faculty room, for instance. Imagine Elizabeth Taylor in National Velvet, showing up in bobbysocks. Who'd notice the socks?

There are laws against petting the teacher's pet and the consequences for anyone crazy enough to break them are uniquely nasty. If an affair with a student came wrapped in a package, the warning label would read: DO NOT OPEN! The big red label on my package said: THIS IN NOT AN AFFAIR! You could say I was lucky not to have been exposed while I was still in town, so to speak. Just imagine the scenario: the devolution of my reputation, the shame dumped on my family, the dirty gossip about "the slut." "They fucked inside the school building," they'd whisper, even though we never fucked, there.

Are you what you do, or what others say about what you do, or what you think about what you have done after the fact? It's hard to measure one's life by bugaboos, and who's to know them better than one's self, but how else? How would you feel if your whole life were about to be recast based on the reactions of just one fellow fumbling through just one folder in just one bottom drawer of your life?

At any rate, that's what I hope dear Kevin thinks about as he fingers those tender envelopes kept so long in my desk drawer. After all the coffees we shared in the lounge during free periods, after the heart-to-heart talks about how he should proceed with his life of exuberant doubt, after his confessions of anxious attraction to Donna Donnabella, the fifteen-year-old heart-throb from over near Mogador, and his desire to break with his father's insistent image of him as a big city corporate lawyer, and more, you'd hope he could be understanding, forgiving even, of his old mentor, snatched away in the midst of his silver years...but you never know what your trusted friends will do, especially when you aren't there.

Kevin came to Green Ravine fresh from graduate school in the Midwest. He was teaching, he said, until he could figure out what to do about a few things, like his fiancee from Ann Arbor, his father's expectations, and his application to law school. He also said he wanted to hike the Appalachian Trail, crew a sail boat to Bermuda from Newport and live on a farm in Vermont. There were other things, as I recall, but from the first day, Kevin was teacher material wrapped in the body of a college lacrosse midfielder and blessed with the baritone voice of a radio disc jockey. His only problem was that he rarely saw the same image twice in the mirror. I, for one, viewed him with a smoldering but benign envy. This guy could fuck the world, if he only wanted to.

As far as the stick-in-the-mud, veteran faculty, we could see that Kevin was probably too restless and too talented to stay at Green Ravine for long, but that goes to show you what we knew. Kevin found challenge and comfort at Green Ravine, and as he got more and more involved with the students through his after-hours coaching and tutoring, he fast became a fixture in the school and the community at large. He was immediately likeable. He played basketball with the kids after school. He volunteered to fill in for lunch duty and bus-loading watch. Parents sang Kevin's praises. Students treated him with kindness and respect, rare at Green Ravine. On his 27th birthday the history club greeted Kevin at the school house doors with a strawberry-chocolate cake baked in the shape of a heart. For his 30th birthday, the lacrosse team gave Kevin a midfielder's stick engraved with their signatures. The faculty and administration realized they had a poster boy in Kevin. The school board instituted an annual award in his name for excellence in teaching. The students voted him "Best Teacher" three years running.

When Kevin slid into the side-chair in my office that one Friday after school to confess his feelings for Donna Donnabella, I vowed to keep his confidences — as well I might, since long-buried memories of my own indiscretions in very similar circumstances sprang back to life. All these years later, I cringe at the memory of myself leaning forward to hear Kevin's anguished emotions. Of all the people he should have talked with about teacher-student love, and lusting after minors! I feel guilty excitement just thinking about it. Like, he was describing her ample ass swaying across the soccer field, and I'm thinking "Don't open that package!" You know, a redder ribbon never wrapped a healthier bum, and poor Kevin's guts were just tied in knots. I did manage to warn him about certain consequences and being courageous in the face of amorous temptation and all of that baloney. He pulled himself together with a round of laughter and snorted on his way out, "Yeah, right!"

She and I spent a June weekend at her father's cottage on Cape Cod. We both figured it was time to talk about what we were going to do about our situation. Sneaking around was an adventure for her, but it was exhausting me. I was learning the hard way that a wife and family didn't make room for real-world dalliances, and the dalliance turned out to have family ties of her own. Her father was at the cottage, which stunned me at the time. Breathing in the stale cigarette smoke of the man, I nearly choked. For that first moment at the screen door, I felt sure to be swept away by a gust of awkwardness. We managed a couple of lemonades. He smoked Chesterfields, one after the other. His ankles were giving him lots of trouble with stiffness, which he suspected was a symptom of arthritis. I saw in the pendulum rise and fall of his hand from ash tray to lips a warning that soon enough I too would be sitting on a porch somewhere, smoking cigarettes and thinking about this time. When she came out after unpacking and changing into white shorts and a loose tank top, relief lifted me into a cloud of brown eyes, and ecstasy flitted about.

That night she played the baby grand piano, night sea breeze flew the curtains in the open windows while I accompanied her on "Edelweiss" and "On The Street Where You Live" before she cruised through the song book of Broadway's best. We lolled against each other for a while before our first goodnight kiss that was actually a good night kiss. We slid off the piano bench and headed down the short hallway to the bedrooms opposite each other.

Lying stiffly on the narrow bed, I felt the lust that had driven me for months drain from my loins as sure as if I'd been catheterized. Unspecified fear seeped into me as I rolled onto my side and closed my eyes. Her father's snoring gasped through the walls until my full retreat into sleep.

The foggy morning light hurt my eyes. Her father's coffee stung my tongue, but I sipped at the brim of the mug until I got used to it. He fumbled around in the deep sink with a certain methodical washing and rinsing hand jive. He didn't say much, but he acted happy enough. His daughter acted lighthearted, too, and maybe that was why he seemed happy. But surely he must have known what I surely knew: that whatever was going on between his daughter and me was about to go nowhere, fast, and that's really why he was acting happy. At the time, I felt like poking the bastard in the eye, but I came to see it his way, eventually. Nothing was said then, or later, when I saw him one more time at her graduation. What words could have found us then?

There's some wisdom beyond the grave, and some empathy, but it's a fool's paradise, too. You can't reach out with words or put a timely arm around a needy shoulder. Kevin was in a tough spot. Given that he'd chewed his guts while waiting for Donna Donnabella to graduate high school before professing his feelings for her, and that he'd pined all the time she was away at college, it's no wonder I grew to respect him so much. I couldn't hold my fire beyond the next spark and pile of dry leaves, whereas Kevin kept himself in check for years, waiting for Donna Donnabella to marry him and make a family home with him. And, I can tell you, his intense integrity worried the hell out of me. What would he do with the damning evidence that revealed his trusted mentor as a chameleon ruled by his peccadilloes, rather than being the leopard of his ethical teachings?

The memorial service trumped all my worries for a while. Cars filled the school parking lots; the overflow packed the shoulder of Route 77 for a quarter mile in both directions. You'd think they were offering free pizza. Dignitaries from the State Legislature to the school board attended. The chaplain of Hobart and William Smith College guided the proceedings with a couple of touching prayers, but the only speaker I listened to was Kevin.

"Bernie was a happy teacher," he began with a deep sigh. "Students responded to his love of learning and his quick wit. He treated them as if they mattered, and he worked tirelessly to show students how rewarding a life of the mind could be. Math was the most difficult subject for Green Ravine's best and brightest, and they entered Bernie's classroom with a volatile mix of dread and determination. Bernie magically, it seems, turned these ingredients into a recipe for fun. For his talents, Bernie was rewarded a thousand times over by adoring and thankful students who would never fear math again, or view the man at the head of the classroom as an adversary."

Kevin paused so long at this point that several people in the packed auditorium began to clap politely, but when Kevin remained anchored behind the podium, all noise quickly faded. Kevin looked out over the crowded rows of upturned faces. His intake of breath alerted even the SRO crowd leaning against the back walls that the next words would be poignant, and true.

"Some of you may know that I fell in love with one of my students, a long time ago. If it were not for Bernie, listening to me, consoling me, yes, and encouraging me to follow my heart's desire, I might very well have lost the greatest love of my life, my Donna — and my two beautiful children. Because of Bernie's confidence in me to do what was best, I was able to abide my heart, without making a mess of my life, or the life of anyone else. Because Bernie was there for me, I was able to be there for Donna all those years when she didn't know I needed her, and now we're there for each other."

A chorus of applause rolled through the hall. Then, Kevin had his last say:

"There are others like me who Bernie counseled toward better choices, better lives. The funny thing is, we are all bound together by Bernie, but we don't know each other by name. Bernie kept our confidences, and I'm sure I'm not the only one who will be forever grateful."

Some day, Kevin will take those words to his own grave, believing in them even as they morph into legendary tales traded across draft beers in taverns around this county for a good long time. Kevin's eulogy humbled me. After the dread and doubt I suffered all through the memorial ceremony, and the soon-to-follow specter of Kevin reading those old letters, you can imagine the feelings that swept over me not 24 hours later.

Kevin unlocked my office door, sat at the desk and pulled the folder from the bottom drawer. Without so much as noting a return address, he fed the flimsy pages into the whine of the shredder, one sheet after another, until they were all gone.

ARTIE'S PLACE

Artie Comstock's house sat half a mile back from Allegheny on a narrow dirt road called Ganson's Lane. The house was the sole survivor of half a dozen structures on the old Ganson farm that ran half-way across the lower township to where it met a long arcing bank of a shallow creek. Artie's place sat in a depression like an afterthought, a couple of stories high at its pitched roof line. A shed roof covered the whole front porch under towering elms that straddled the little house. Artie passed a lot of time rocking back and forth on that porch from where he could watch the old Ganson track sprout side- hall Colonials and double-dormered Capes from three-acre lots that sold at a steady pace to urban family types who thought country living would be good for their children's health and education.

Artie was a favorite patient of mine. He only called when he needed a doctor. On a house call I made one spring, Artie was bound up with some kind of ailment of the lower intestine, and we tried damned near everything to get him functioning, but I could only do so much at his house, and I wanted him to go to the hospital where we could administer 24-hour treatment and do diagnostic tests that would tell us if surgery might be a viable alternative. The most difficult thing I have to do as a doctor is convince an unwilling patient to go to the hospital. "Unwilling" in Artie's case puts it mildly. He finally agreed, but I had to promise to drive him into Batavia myself. He didn't have much to pack, and I had several patients to see in the hospital already, so waiting a few minutes for Artie to get himself together gave me time for a little rocking on that sunny porch.

On the ride in, Artie was nervous as hell, and I figure that's why he talked so much. I wasn't nervous at all, of course, and I confess to a keen interest in whatever Artie had to say. He was that kind of guy.

Turns out Artie was born a free black man in Newport, Rhode Island, where his father was a manager in the shipping business he'd established some time before the turn of the century. Artie's father was born free, and so was his grandfather. Artie had moved west to take up farming against his father's wishes, and to hear him tell it, Artie's father never forgave him and never offered to help him when things didn't turn out as planned. Artie apparently had a difficult time convincing bankers to loan him enough money to finance a potato-growing venture, and he got caught in cycles of credits and debts that finally drove him into bankruptcy, followed by years of subsistence farming. Although Artie spent much of his adult life striving and failing at the farm business, he was proud of his status. "I was born free, Doc, and I'm gonna die free, too."

The hospital stay worked out well for Artie. We were able to get his bowels working without surgery; the long term diagnosis wasn't particularly good news as Artie had some colitis and a few other problems I didn't like the looks of. We talked with an oncologist at Roswell and a Rochester internist about Artie's chances of having a slow growing cancer. Artie was older than he looked, and his skill at distracting doctors from their duties over the years had not produced a reliable medical history. In fact, I got confused more than once between what seemed to be Artie's history and what sounded like the saga of a restless soul. Just the same, my patient was looking some serious medical problems in the eye, and if that didn't put him on notice of a physical life he was in fact living, I didn't know what I could do about it.

What he did almost as soon as he got home from the hospital strikes me now as irrational, but who's to say? Artie adopted a mutt that had lost his left front leg, just below the knee, to a mowing machine, the blade nipping off his lower leg as he dodged away not quite fast enough to save his leg but fast enough to save his life. The dog and Artie bonded immediately. Artie fed the dog pork chops for dinner. He taught the dog tricks that made the short leg work like a paw. The dog could point, count and "shake hands." But the strangest thing the dog could do was yowl like he was talking. People came by to see the 3-legged talking dog. It was worth the silver coins they often dropped into the little tin bank strung from the dog's collar.

Maybe all those paying visitors got Artie to thinking about moving into town, where he could become a tourist attraction. I don't know, stranger things have happened, but I've got to say, Artie's attempts to move into town gave rise to the nastiest town politics I've been a part of, before or since.

It seems that Artie had his eye on a rather lonely-looking house that sat squarely in the middle of downtown. The house needed new clapboards and lots of fresh paint, plus a window pane or two, and plans for the condemnation and sale of the property were passed into a resolution by the village zoning board. The plans called for one last attempt at selling the property, and a ridiculously low price was advertised. Everyone considered the place a dump and figured the next call would go out for a bulldozer. To the surprise of all involved, two bids for the property came in under the deadline. A shopping mall developer from Marion, Ohio tendered the first bid. One Arthur J. Comstock submitted the other at a higher offer. Each bid was backed by a bank-certified deposit. The zoning board held an open meeting, as required by law, to discuss the bids and what to do next. Usually, the high bidder would get the property, and that would be that, but it didn't turn out that way. A board member moved to table the decision in lieu of further research.

Marj came home from that meeting in a rage that shocked the hell out of me. I'd never seen her so upset. She kept yelling at no one in particular, "He's black, that's why!" After she settled down and told me about the meeting, I started to get the picture, and even though I didn't like it, I thought there must be some kind of misunderstanding. Maybe the town board was worried about a developer coming in and redesigning the downtown, ruining what was left of its 19th Century charm.

At church the following Sunday, our minister sermonized about the plight of the Southern Negro and the God-given courage it would take to bring about fairness and justice. I noticed very few parishioners stopping by to shake his hand at the door on their way out of the church. Looking back at it now, I should have seen it as a sign that many in our cozy, northern town feared the specter of change flashing across our TV screens from places like Selma and Birmingham.

I went to the next zoning board meeting myself. I attend more meetings than I like to, being on the staff at three hospitals, doing the county home job and coroner's duties. Many meetings are tightly run by agendas and Robert's Rules of Order, or their many approximations. This particular meeting warped into a shouting match within minutes. People who had grown up with each other yelled at the top of their lungs, tone deaf to their friends, oblivious to any protocols of order. Artie Comstock, a long-standing member of our community, was vilified as a rabble-rousing, "civil rights ingratiate" who would be "ridden out of town on a rail" if not for the hideous laws protecting "niggers" from their "just deserts." I stood to speak and went unrecognized and unnoticed for at least ten minutes. A lull in the mayhem finally came, but I found no voice in my throat. I slinked home, defeated in a way I couldn't really comprehend or explain.

Two additional public meetings produced little more than vitriolic chaos and no decision on the downtown property. The out-of-town developer backed out, eventually, and Artie Comstock's bid expired after the 60-day claim period. The property itself stood empty, and stands empty to this day, looking more and more like the symbol of a community without purpose.

It's a tough realization, coming to see that the golden world you live in turns out to be a mirage. All the blood I've seen is red. That's how I know people as pretty much the same for my purposes, but lots of others don't think or feel that way. Around here, Artie's blood was black. Whether he was descended from free Blacks, like half a million other Black people in America's history, or not, made no difference to anyone but Artie. I worked on that idea for a lot of driving miles over the next several weeks, and I can't say I really got it straightened out, but I did have a sort of epiphany along about West Batavia one night: God would give it more time.

Artie's case simmered. Marj juggled the music and sports schedules of our kids, and I think it helped keep her mind off the issues of what she called "small-town-small-mind," and I'll omit the noun. I kept busy with one thing and another. Months melted by while I attended to the various health needs of patients. I was simply clicking along like you do during those periods of worry-free routine: you get plenty to eat, you sleep when you want, your friends get along and no long-lost relatives show up asking for money.

•   •   •   •   •

I was cruising along Allegheny, headed for home, thinking nothing in particular about anything, when Ganson Lane came up just ahead to my left. I hit the brakes and turned in. Somebody had paved the road, widened it and put in shoulders all the way back to Artie's place. The new houses that had looked so out of place a few months before actually appeared to fit into the land. Landscaping and a few rooting trees did wonders. Even Artie's wore a fresh coat of white paint. The late afternoon sun gave the place a welcoming glow.

The people milling around on the porch came into focus as I drove closer. They were dressed in dark suits. I recognized one of Artie's sons. When I got out of the car, I walked up to the steps and said hello. I was just driving by and I wanted to stop in and see how Artie was doing.

"He'd love to see you, Doc. A little late, is all."

Artie's place wasn't much of a house. Small kitchen in the back, a keeping room attached. Dining room, sitting room, stairs cut along the wall to two bedrooms upstairs. I took off my hat and stepped inside the dim light of the sitting room. Artie lay on the dining room table. He was decked out in a blue gabardine suit, polished wing tips, paisley tie, and trimmed salty hair. A set of mauve colored pillows propped his head, and a hand-stitched quilt lay beneath him and fell over the edges of the table. The dining room chairs lined the walls of the sitting room. My feet stuck to the floor boards.

"Wanna bury Dad in his garden out back, Doc. There's probably a law against it."

I'd been the county coroner for 25 years, and I didn't know exactly what the law said about home burials, but I knew I didn't want to know, either.

Marj went with me to Artie's burial in the garden. Besides the strong west wind, it was a decent day. I stared at the turned earth of the fallow garden and thought about the tectonic shifts happening in our culture and how all the marches on Washington, the burning cities, the inspired speeches wouldn't impress Artie much. He'd waited a long time to be caught up with, and he was just plain tired out. Besides he was born free, lived free, and died free. What more could a good man ask?

WHAT I WANT TO SAY

The summer I turned 12, my parents decided to send me to YMCA Camp so I could practice being on my own. I suspected they really wanted to be free of me for a while. All of a sudden, it seemed, I was bunking in a one-room cabin with long wooden shutters for windows, straw mattresses slung on iron springs, and spider webs the size of kites strung from the roof beams. Late, after the other 9 boys sputtered into sleep, I lay flat in my sleeping bag, wondering who I would be friends with during the summer.

Howie Sampson looked like he was etched out of dark wood, but his cheekbones, elbows, knees, and knuckles were as smooth as tanned hide. When he boxed, his hands cuffed and slapped like paws, punching with punishing economy. It turned out Howie was a real live orphan sponsored at the Y Camp by the Batavia Chapter of Kiwanis. Howie was what my father would call "unfortunate in his choice of parents."

Howie bunked with the other kids in the special Kiwanis building close to the mess hall. One of the kids was wheel-chair bound; three were blind; one little boy was missing a hand and both feet. It became easy to call the Kiwanis campers names, because most of them didn't care or notice. "Pork Chop," "Flat Head," "Shit-for-Brains."

Howie avoided activities involving other Kiwanis campers, and when he ate at their assigned tables he kept his head down, acting sullen. He wouldn't pass the salt; he seemed not to hear "please" or "thank you." And, worst of all, he refused to bus his own dirty dishes.

Wise-guy counselors teased him at first, but soon enough they started asking him if he "would mind," or if he "would like to…" Anybody who called him "Little Red Man" to his face got punched. Sometimes Howie would spit at you; it didn't matter who you were. The bigger guys steered clear of him because the camp director usually blamed them for starting trouble; the smaller guys were simply scared of him. As the days passed, I could see that Howie was running a sort of camp within the camp, and I disliked him for it as much as I envied him.

That was twenty-three years ago. Now, the YMCA Camp is defunct, up for sale. I bounced around for awhile after community college before finding the perfect fit for me. I'm a realtor working for a big upstate broker in my hometown where the business is steady and my roots are deep. I drove out from Batavia to meet a client who's flying in from Nebraska to see if the boys' camp he runs can be moved to New York State. I park my Blazer at the top of the overgrown camp grounds that slope all the way to the lake below.

The mess hall sets parallel to the road, woodbine and sumac climbing over the rotting eaves. Washed-out paint peels from the door and window frames, and the well-worn paths to the front doors I remember so keenly are all but gone to the weeds. The Kiwanis building is boarded up; the latrine and outdoor wash basins have been dismantled. I'm not sure I want to trek up to the playing fields, but from where I stand you can't distinguish the baseball diamond from the soccer field. Only the rusty chain-linked boundary fences mark the basketball and tennis courts. If the place were closer to town, a developer would see a lot of potential for a nice townhouse community with a knockout view. This Nebraska guy would need deep pockets — and a good marketing plan.

From up here, I can make out the weathered roofs of a few cabins, shaded by towering maples. A smattering of elms have survived and stand like sentinels above the terraced common park area of the camp where we were called to morning calisthenics by the tinny-sounding bugle over the campus loud speaker system. Without fully intending to, I walk down to the heart of the camp, memories and stories pinging in my mind.

Howie spent his free mornings fishing, and out of curiosity I decided to join him. Howie sat half-way out on a limb over the lake; he dangled a rod from the crook of his arm while humming a tune I didn't recognize. I didn't think he noticed me squatting at the base of the tree, watching him.

"Saw you comin' out of the corner of my eye, white boy."

He reeled in the line and swung the hook into his hand. "Lost another worm."

He dug a night crawler from the tin can and dangled it toward me. "Long and skinny like me, same color too."

"You're not purple," I said, matter of fact.

"What do you know, white boy?" He tossed the worm in the air, caught it, and stitched the hook through it. He whipped the pole overhand; the hook and line snagged in a branch.

"You should have cast side-arm," I said.

"Shit! Messed up my concentration! Should kick you in the ass!"

Howie hopped down just as Big Ed Tucker, camp director, passed by on his morning patrol. He made my father look like a teddy bear; any campers who crossed Tucker didn't get a second chance at it.

"Foul language is against the YMCA code, boys. You know that. Tell me, what's going on here? Why aren't you attending classes this morning?"

Howie looked at Tucker's feet and said nothing.

Tucker glared so hard I thought a fire would explode in Howie's hair.

I answered questions while Howie played dumb. Fishing was apparently forbidden without a camp counselor present, especially during morning classes. Tucker took me by the arm, guiding me toward the canoe class.

Howie shot me the finger when Tucker wasn't looking, then he climbed back into the tree.

The big willow is gone; the shoreline is filled in with reeds and muck. The beach could use a load of sand. Up at the camp-fire site, I kick around in the dirt with the same slow feet that failed me in a bout with Howie in the old days. Howie boxed every day, and it was right about where I'm standing that he turned eager beavers into woodchucks with his phantom moves and flicking punches. No matter where you were on the waterfront, you could hear the hyped action around the out-door ring. "Howie! Howie! Howie!" I used to stand on a log so I could watch him; I figured there must be a way to beat him.

There was a husky red-head from cabin 6 who chased Howie around the ring until he exhausted himself, then Howie used him for a punching bag. A tough-talking freckled kid from Oakfield hated Howie for towel-snapping in the shower. He challenged Howie to a match almost daily, but every match ended the same way: the kid's bruises got darker, his lips fatter, his fury spent.

Randy Quilts, tall and broad-shouldered, was another matter altogether. His blond crew-cut glowed in the afternoon sunlight as it poured down through the high trees. Randy's bright orange boxing gloves blossomed with power as he snapped punch after punch. Randy exuded confidence — some said arrogance — but he liked to show other guys how to hold their hands and swing from a balanced stance. He showed me a few things, and just for fun, he set me up for a bout with Howie. I'd imagined boxing Howie, but I didn't actually want to box Howie. I pretended it was no big deal, but inside, I was terrified.

Howie decoyed me for a round to make sure I couldn't get near him. Oh, I tried, swinging wildly, chasing him, grazing his arms a couple of times. Howie was really crafty, a constantly moving target. After the second round, I could barely catch my breath. Early in the third round, I became Howie's punching bag du jour. His punches blurred in my face, and I ducked into an uppercut. End of fight. I sat in the dust, listening to the time keeper bang the old kettle while a small crowd of campers sang "bye-bye, birdie" off key. Randy and Howie walked off in different directions. I got up, brushed myself off and feeling no pain (except the kind that's invisible), went for a swim.

There was quite a collection of us, a kind of club of Howie's victims, who chided his restless and roaming ways and made fun of him whenever we could — from a distance. My own curiosity continued and was shortly rewarded when I came upon Howie sitting cross-legged in a secluded section of shoreline at the camp boundary. He looked like a brave from the movie Broken Arrow. I asked him what he was doing, even though I could see he was whittling a long stick.

"Making a whip to beat wild pigs in the ass."

I wanted to smash him, but it wouldn't be fair to hit someone who was sitting down. Not even foul-mouthed Howie.

"How would you like to be my buddy for general swim?"

"I ain't nobody's buddy."

"It's just for swimming. You can swim, can't you?"

My father couldn't make Father's Weekend at Camp because he had to work. It seemed no one else's father had to work, so I took some comfort from the big man voices of other fathers booming through the woods. The wide-bodied men bounding off the swimming docks broke some strict rules we boys were held to. Weekend fathers recruited from the First National Bank, Sylvania, Montgomery Ward, and other local businesses attended the weekend to be with the Kiwanis "boys without Dads." The three blind mice got a lot of attention, as did the kid we called "Shit-for-Brains." Howie kept to himself. Ball games, boat races, archery competitions, ping-pong tournaments and talent shows ran all weekend, but it was the culminating event on Sunday afternoon that got everybody together. The pig roasted on a spit, and the undefeated boxers for the whole summer were hot to duke it out in the campfire ring.

The Randy Quilts vs. Howie Sampson bout was refereed and judged by Big Ed Tucker. The format was simple: three 3-minute rounds, separated by one minute breaks.

Randy wore white satin trunks trimmed in red. His father unwrapped cordovan-colored leather boxing shoes, held them up for the gathering crowd to see, then laced them up for his son. When Randy popped up from the three-legged stool at the edge of the ring, he looked like an Olympic champ.

Howie, round-shouldered, wearing cut-off jeans and canvas sneaks, shadow-boxed across the ring. I counted Howie's ribs and wondered what would happen if Randy caught him moving the wrong way.

Tucker waved both boxers into center ring. "Let's have a good fight," he barked, and the boxers touched gloves.

Randy tapped Howie in the nose at the break and grazed him with an elbow. The next punch looked low, but everyone jumped up in front of me, and all I saw was a dust cloud rising above the fighters. I moved to an open slot where a gang of fathers, sitting on a log, leaned over their knees.

Howie moved at top speed, slipping punch after punch from Randy's shining gloves. Two minutes into the round, Randy caught Howie on the temple, slowing him enough to land two hard body punches. Howie bobbed and weaved, covering up. Randy squared up and pounded him; Howie slid away. Randy cut off the ring, cornering Howie.

"PATIENCE!" Randy's father yelled above the noise. You could see the Quilts' strategy: sap Howie's speed, then attack him without the danger of a counter-attack.

At the bell, Howie took a punch below the belt and doubled over. Randy pranced over to his stool to get a cool sponge-down and some Vaseline spread around his eyes. Tucker leaned over Howie and told him he could forfeit due to injury. "Nuh,uh," Howie muttered and stood up to stretch and swing his arms. By the bell for round 2, Howie was bouncing on his toes, and Tucker waved the boxers into the center of the ring.

Randy threw a combination, Howie wheeled backward, looking for room, Randy pursued, bollo punching, kicking up dirt. The deafening noise gaves the camp fire ring the feel of an arena. Then, Howie broke free, but he didn't get his hands up in time to block Randy's hook to the chin. WHAM! Howie hit the ground. Tucker pushed Randy toward his corner and went back to pump his arm over Howie. At the count of eight, Howie wobbled to his feet; Randy bull-rushed Howie to finish the job, but Tucker held him back with a warning. Howie glided away, Quilts yelled, "INTERFERENCE," amid a wave of boos.

Randy closed for the kill. Howie watched him come across the ring and stutter-stepped, faked right. Randy anticipated and moved to block him, then, Howie faked left, turning Randy a half step into his quick right hand.

"Eat that!"

"PASTE THAT LITTLE BASTARD!" Quilts got everybody roaring.

Randy charged again, but Howie side-stepped him, tapping him twice on the way by. Randy wheeled around to get him, but instead of backpedaling, Howie waded in, flailing with both hands, driving Randy backward into the crowd.

The timekeeper banged the kettle furiously as Tucker separated the boxers and sent them to their respective corners. Randy got his Vaseline touch-up and sponge bath along with his father's pep talk, but in the other corner, Howie sagged like a rag doll. His gloves were loose, his left sneaker untied. His eyes searched the crowd until they found me. "Corner Man," he mouthed, motioning me to come.

I jumped between two fathers and ran to him. I got his gloves tightened and his sneaker tied. He had a welt on his forehead and blood trickling from his nose. He let me dab him with a wet handkerchief, and I talked into his ear: "Clinch and upper-cut." Howie stared across the ring at Randy and Mr. Quilts. For a split second, I wished Dad were there. Then the bell rattled, and Howie took a couple of steps forward.

Randy rushed straight across the ring, grazing Howie's head as he ducked. Then Randy missed with a short right, Howie slipping by, landing a hard kidney punch.

"DON'T LET HIM DO THAT!" Quilts yelled.

Randy whirled after Howie, gloved him by the neck and threw him down. Before Tucker could jump between the fighters, Randy kicked dirt in Howie's face.

"ALL RIGHT!" Quilts roared above the crowd.

Howie staggered to his feet; Randy crowded close with both hands pumping; Howie tied him up, pulling Randy in a circle. As they broke, Howie's upper-cut dinged Randy's chin. Two fast jabs and an over-hand right sprang between Randy's gloves.

The blows electrified the crowd. Even though Howie looked like a dirty sheet hanging in the wind, he was fighting with courage and skill. I felt sudden pride for coaching the clinch and upper-cut tactic. Randy stepped back far enough to regroup and shake his head clear. Mr. Quilts howled in pure frustration:

PUT THIS NIGGER IN THE TANK, AND LET'S EAT SOME PORK!" It was dead silent for a time. Then another father growled, "Yeah, we're gettin' hungry!" Laughter broke out.

I felt myself getting crazy mad.

Howie spat on the ground halfway between Randy and Mr. Quilts and pointed a glove at each of them. Randy tore after Howie. Howie counter-punched, sticking Randy consistently until Randy was weeping blood onto his white satin shorts. Randy threw a left-right combination, then missed a round-house, leaving him off-balance. Howie pounced into the opening with a stunning flurry of punches; Randy fell. Howie spat on him, then kicked him in the balls.

Tucker couldn't move fast enough to stop Mr. Quilts from grabbing Howie's throat, and then it took Tucker's full strength to pull me off Mr.Quilts, at whom I flailed for all I was worth.

The big pines made a kind of natural cathedral in which simple benches faced a carved, walnut altar. I went there to pray and to wait for an answer about what I should do. Tucker had already called my father and asked him to come and get me, for I'd been expelled from camp. I sat in the dark, facing the altar, feeling like I should get on my knees, but also feeling like having an argument with whoever God was.

"Wha-choo want, white boy?"

I turned toward his voice. Howie was barely visible in the pale dark. I said my father was coming tomorrow; he'd be mad as hell.

Howie looked like a shadow coming nearer along the front row of benches.

"I'm going to cut you, give me your hand." He spewed foul breath into my face and pressed the knife blade flat against my neck.

I froze.

"You're a Mohawk for the rest of your earthly life."

I flinched as he grabbed my hand, brought the blade down from my neck and slashed the palm of my left hand, all in one motion. Then, Howie smeared the oozing blood from my hand against the oozing blood from his hand.

"Tell your daddy you did it for your own."

I remember the next day clear as a bell: Howie leaning against the mess hall door, my father spinning the car wheels as he tore down the camp driveway, heading for home. About a mile from the camp, Dad accused me of being a disgrace to the family name, a disgrace to him as a man. He called me things I'd never heard before as he waved the form Tucker asked him to sign relieving the "YMCA Inc." from responsibility in the "unfortunate incident involving your son." There was no way to tell my father what had really happened, or why I felt like fighting.

Tripping the door handle and pushing hard against the wind, I threw myself out of the car.

When I came to in the hospital two days later, Dad was pacing at the foot of the bed. He didn't notice me watching him through the bandage over my left eye. I watched him cry when he left the room.

After I returned home, my father acted uncomfortable when we were alone together, and I often met his eyes with my own mixed emotions. In my darker moods, I imagined my empty eye socket staring at him in his dreams.

That whole year was a blur for me, and when I heard Howie got transferred out of the Batavia Home for Boys, I was relieved that he wouldn't be turning up at any Y-Camp reunions.

It wasn't long before I got my driver's license, one eye and all, and got to drive my own junker without needing to ask my father for his car. Maybe Dad and I would have had the talks we needed to have if we'd ridden together during his later years and my more tolerant ones. I think about that a lot.

So, here I am, watching the guy from Nebraska amble down the hill from where he's parked his rented Firebird next to my Blazer. As he gets closer, I see his bony nose, the graying temples, the deep crow's feet running into his hairline. It's Howie. I know it's him, and I know, too, that he doesn't recognize me. I'm ready to shake hands, but he jerks his arm up in an open-hand salute. "Peace be with you, friend."

I just stand in the space between two big trees as he walks past me a few steps toward the lake.

"The old place hasn't changed much," he says. "It's really good of you to come all the way out here to meet me." He turns to face me. "My boys call me 'The Rev', short for the right Reverend Howard Everett Sampson." He nods and chuckles to himself, and we proceed along the widening pathway to the waterfront, Howie a couple steps ahead of me.

"Just call me Bill," I say. "My broker tells me you used to be a Y-Camper."

"Oh, yes, a long time ago, a long time ago. I was one ornery son-of-a-gun back then, headed for a godless, no-good end.

You could have called me the Devil's Misery Stew!" He addressed the high, overhanging trees as if he were in an amphitheater, and I wondered where he'd learned the smooth talk.

"Yessir, down here, I swung 'n' punched, got swung at, punched too, knocked senseless more than once. But if it weren't for the laying on of those hands, I doubt I would have ever become aware of the almighty Jesus Christ. Humph, humph, like a combination to the head and heart, simultaneously. It was right here in this YMCA Camp that The Reverend Howard Everett Sampson was reborn.

"Oh, that fighting, that darn ol' fighting. Is that how you lost your eye, Mr. Bill? Fighting?"

Maybe it's a religious experience, returning to a place where you buried part of yourself as a child. That pebble waits for you to come back so you can dig up a stone. Across the palm of my hand, the faint white scar where Howie drew the knife that night crosses my life line. I run my finger tip along the two lines, then scratch my eye patch reflexively. Dad died 13 years ago, but this weird turn of events brings back the fear that my father will disown me.

The Rev has been poking along the overgrown shoreline where the sandy beach used to be. He turns and comes back toward where I'm standing near the old fire pit. The lake spreads out behind him, making him look taller than he actually is.

"Okay," he says, "this is a special place, a hallowed place; I'll meet the asking price. Can we shake on it?

"I don't know why not," I say, and extend my hand.

THAT MAN

Taciturn, that's Frank, keeps pretty much to himself, although he's pleasant enough when you run into him at the store or the bank.

His wife, Beverly, or "Sunny" as we call her, is preternaturally bright. She projects an inner glow, and she's very compassionate where other people are concerned.

Couples like Frank and Sunny Ruddick can keep their union functioning simply by the tension of their opposition. The balance works fairly well until one or more children come into the family. Then competition for control can get spinning, and everybody loses. I've seen any number of children play one parent against the other for advantage, or maybe just for amusement, but some children actually inherit a mean streak from somewhere, and that can ruin a family. Jason Ruddick fit into that category. Expressly.

Jason could apply his meanness in a kind of brilliant concentration on the football field, and I watched him win at least two games for the high school team last fall on plays only he could have made. In one game deep in our own territory, he sprinted under a pass that appeared to be lofting perfectly to the opposing receiver: Interception. In the other game, Jason stole a Hail Mary pass by out-leaping three opponents for the ball. Since he was the only defender, it was quite a play. How he came up with that catch is a wonder to me, even now. After each of those plays was over, Jason shoved the ball into the face of an opposing player. The referee levied personal fouls against him (and the team, of course), but Jason proudly stalked to the sidelines like a little prince.

Frank screamed bloody murder from the bleachers, calling the refs all kinds of names.

During the winter exam week, Jason aced three advanced Regents exams, thus winning scholarships to any state college of his choice. He also got recruiting letters from several colleges in New England and two private liberal arts colleges in central New York. Sunny couldn't stop crowing about Jason's academic achievements. She threw a celebration party and drove a carload of his classmates to the Knox-Albright Museum in Buffalo during winter break.

As far as I know, Frank never said a word to anyone about Jason's scholarships.

Pee Wee Clark didn't have a mean bone in his body, or in his head. In fact, he even made me feel mean when I had to kick him off the front porch during office hours one time. He was disturbing some of my patients with his foul booze breath and that glazy, bloodshot look in his eyes. When he gave me his poor little sheep-dog expression, I hesitated; then I noticed the slobber in his chin whiskers. That was it.

"Go ahead, Pee Wee, get about your business somewhere else."

He sauntered off, I went back inside, and wouldn't you know, ol' Pee Wee turned up at the back door, where Marj fixed him a thick ham and cheese sandwich with iced tea and potato chips on the side. Probably the only real food he'd eaten in three days. "Aw, hi Doc," he mumbled, full-mouthed, a mischievous energy in his eyes.

Pee Wee lived in a chicken shack with his friend and fellow wastrel, "Chub." Chub didn't get around much, unlike Pee Wee who roamed the village streets at all hours, relentless as he was harmless. During the early afternoons, Pee Wee knocked on doors and offered his lawn-raking and tree-trimming services in exchange for a little spending money. Before his life fell apart, he'd worked hard labor on the outlying farms during harvest, but that was back in the days before I'd even started practicing medicine here. As the story goes, he was one of the area's most promising young men in his day. He graduated with honors in Engineering from Union before he flew fighter missions in the War.

Pee Wee's hero status bought him drinks all over Western New York. His first marriage was highlighted by a congratulatory citation from President Truman, and when he opened Clark Builders, Inc., he could hardly keep up with the demand for his services, but somewhere along the line, he lost the business during a wrongful death lawsuit involving a foreman who'd hired two migrant workers. The migrants claimed they knew all about scaffolding; they didn't. The foreman disappeared, Pee Wee paid a huge fine, the company lost its reputation, and that was that. I don't know when the whiskey caught up with him, but that's about the time his wife left town with the last of his money and the remains of his broken heart.

Anyway, the night Pee Wee and Chub got burned up in the chicken shack fire, I was out on a call east of town. A couple of fire engines wailed by, followed by the usual caravan of flashing lights and pick-ups. I dashed to my car and fell in line. The glowing sky was easy to target and everyone pulled in fast to get as close to the blaze as possible.

The fire and explosion had blown the shack to smithereens. Bits of tar paper and shingle littered the long grass and hung in the lower limbs of the apple trees. The firemen got water on the fire quick enough, but there wasn't much to save. Beneath the white hot core of rubble marking the center of the shack, you could make out the steaming humps of what had been, just hours before, two men. I can't describe the smell, but I can't forget it, either.

Pee Wee and Chub were apparently operating a still, which made some sense, in retrospect. How else could they afford 'round-the-clock drinking habits? They made a mistake by selling hooch to local kids, and worse, they groomed Jason Ruddick as their go-between. It must have been easy for them to do business with just one kid, and for the kid, an ever-growing clientele meant growing profits, and increasing power. The trouble was that Jason Ruddick led what you could call a neighborhood gang marked by a constantly expanding appetite for mischief and mayhem. The two bums were easy marks for taunting and stoning.

A farmer, whose name I won't mention, told me he'd watched the gang steal up on the shack the night of the fire. He said it was pretty dark, but he was sure he saw the Ruddick kid throw the first lighted flare onto the roof of the shack. He couldn't see who tossed the other flares that eventually torched the place. "They kept gasoline back there, beside the still, but I wouldn't swear to it. Those two bums didn't have a chance."

By the time the fire got put down, Pee Wee and Chub were cooked. You see sights you don't want to see, let alone remember, but if I live to be a hundred, I won't be able to erase that scene from my memory.

Everybody heard the rumors going around town the next week. People took sides. The minister raised holy hell in our church, and I heard the priest up the street did the same. The local paper covered the fire on page one. The lead editorial scolded the community for fostering children with values "condoning torture and murder!"

It was a Wednesday, busy like you wouldn't believe: allergies, rashes, three cases of impetigo in one family, premature babies in the incubators at the hospital. I slipped into one of those health-care marathons where day and night turn upside down. Cat naps, cold soup, hot coffee, no laughs.

Sunny Ruddick called some time after 10. Frank had gone in to take a bath and he couldn't climb out of the tub. I drove over to their place at the other end of town and hustled up to the second-floor bathroom.

Frank stared up at me from the bath water. "My legs won't move, Doc."

It struck me that Frank Ruddick was reporting the condition of his legs to me, without really feeling connected to them.

Sunny sat on a stool near the rim of the tub; tears streaked her face. I'm standing at the edge of the big porcelain tub. Frank's mostly covered by foamy water.

"Can you wiggle your toes, Frank?"

"Boys will be boys," he said.

I've got to admit I didn't know what he was talking about—not at first. Maybe he was in shock. Traumatic dementia. I asked him, again, if he could move his toes.

"That scum didn't deserve this town."

Sunny slipped out of the bathroom, leaving me to sit on a children's step stool by the tub, deprived of any of the objective information needed for doing my job. I reached for Frank's hand to find a pulse.

He pulled away.

"Water must be getting a little cold by now," I said, and I wondered about what had happened before Frank got into the bath. It was going to be my next question. "Let me help you up, Frank. I'll get under your arms, and you see if you can pull your legs underneath you."

"Never mind, Doc, I don't need you. The patient is downstairs."

Sunny wraps her hands around a mug of tea. I sit across the small kitchen table and try to make eye contact; she won't lift her face to me. "Why did you call, Sunny?" I want a clue, some understanding, while sounding as gentle as possible. Sometimes when you're really tired, you can be really gentle.

"I'm at the end of my rope, Ben."

There's nothing more depressing than sitting with a favorite patient while she unravels. You listen, murmur, grunt, and try to find a way to break the fall.

"Frank was never easy, but we did okay. Jason came along, and life took on some glow; we did everything together. Then Jason got older, and Frank got, I don't know how to say it; does 'gone' do it?"

"Fine," I say.

"Then, this fire incident. Do you know Jason hates school? Doesn't want any part of college, wants to be a professional firefighter. A goddamned fireman! Please, Ben, forgive me."

"Nothing to forgive."

"Those were Frank's flares. He knew Jason would use them, somehow. I'm not sure he didn't dare Jason to throw them at Pee Wee and that other creep."

I was suddenly wide awake, fully alert. I didn't want to hear more, even though I wanted to know more. I held Sunny's hands tight in mine and told her to check on Frank to make sure he didn't drown in the tub. I called for the ambulance from Sunny's kitchen wall phone.

Here was a loving woman losing connection with her husband and dreading visits to her only son in prison. Jason would certainly avoid college, and Frank could avoid Sunny, but she would abide both of them anyway, alone, for the rest of her life. I suppose if crying were a release for me that would have been the night for it.

At the pathologist's autopsy, I stood at the head of the stainless steel table to witness the picking and poking of Pee Wee's remains. The stench of burned flesh clung to the antiseptic, windowless room. I thought of Pee Wee wandering our little town for years, searching for the man he remembered being. He must have been proud of that man.

In his sweetest illusions, he was that man.

GANADO DREAMING

Patty swung her arm back right past my ear and lobbed the ring up into the speckled sky. I listened for the clink out there in the sand, but the cool night air kept the sound to itself. I'd never seen anyone do that before, throw a ring away, a guy's ring he must have given with some piece of his heart in mind.

"That's it for him," she said in a tone just loud enough for me to feel like I was listening in. "He coulda come out here for a coupla weeks; it wouldna killed him."

I leaned against the top rail of the rough fence that marked the outer boundary of Ganado, where the irrigated grass gave way to desert scrub. It was so quiet, you'd think you'd be able to hear a rhinestone ring hit the dirt a few-dozen feet away, but yards could easily become miles and then millennia that swallowed up that lonely square-mile of oasis.

It was one thing to sign up for a summer sojourn on a Presbyterian mission in the southwest and another to stand in the dark desert and think you could hear the stars.

"So, what are you going to tell him when you get back?" I really didn't care all that much, but Patty was pretty steamed up, and I wanted to be careful about not saying the wrong thing in the wrong way.

"Not going back, I never liked Fort Wayne, and I like it less now. Do you know how close we are to California?"

I had some idea, but I sensed she wasn't referring to distance. "You keep heading west, outside Ganado, and I'll bet you could drive it in twelve to fifteen hours, easy."

"Why are you so smart? I'll bet you figure a rate of speed too, in that New York City brain of yours."

I wasn't from New York City, and Patty knew that because I'd gone into a whole explanation about upstate and downstate at the orientation session last Sunday night at the church, but getting caught up in all of that again would just make her angry. That's the last thing I needed.

"You do, don't you, figure stuff like that!"

"Sometimes," I said. "It's fun."

"Fun!"

I felt her staring at me, but I couldn't really see her eyes. The sky was bright, but below the horizon, everything got sucked in. Her breath was almost in my face, and her head shadow was about all I could make out from where she stood.

"Fun," she said again, without so much heat. "Fun," she choked a little, "I don't know if fun is something I could describe as ever having."

"What's his name?" I asked, not knowing what else to say.

"Jim."

"Jim?"

"Just Jim. Jim, Jim, Jimmy."

It was a long, dark walk back to the cavernous dorm where all of the summer volunteers bunked in the quarters of the Navajo high school kids who lived there from September to May. Patty headed straight for the girls' side of the building, and for the next three weeks of her stay, she avoided me like high-altitude chiggers, which was really okay with me. I felt guilty for being in on a secret I didn't want to know, had no reason to keep, and didn't have anyone to tell who would care either.

Abraham Lincoln swung out to the extent of the chain and dropped back down and through to the bottom of the pendulum and up again, passing me going in the opposite direction. We had met on the big swing set the first night of July. His name was a real novelty at first but I got used to it soon enough. "Linc" was a day student, and he took the cafeteria suppers as late as possible so he wouldn't have to drive his old pick-up out to the family hogan until after dark. He knew I wanted to see the place, but it took him time to trust me, even though he was as curious about the Anglo from the east as I was about the Navajo from Arizona.

We bumped and banged along a desert track for what seemed like an hour before a tiny glint of light blossomed into a single yard light on a short pole. Linc coasted the truck to a halt near the light pole and we got out, slamming the creaky doors behind us.

"Home," he said. "Welcome home, hey." Linc hit his one-note chuckle, and I followed him inside.

His mother must have already retired to the bedroom, cut off from the middle of the hogan by a thick rug that hung from a low cross-beam. In the dim light cast from the corner table lamp, the rug's red and black design made shapes like long arrowheads that in the shadowy light, looked like they could be moving.

"Have one." Linc handed me a beer he'd pulled out of a tiny fridge tucked into a cupboard that angled across a corner of the hogan. From the outside, I'd noticed the traditional octagonal structure, but once inside I couldn't orient myself to the layout. It felt bigger than I'd imagined, yet the lack of bright light made me feel claustrophobic. Linc drank his beer in a couple of long gulps, like it was water. He bent into the cupboard for another.

A box of empties stood in the corner close by. A kerosene lamp hung from the central ceiling beam.

Linc saw me looking up at it. "It's good for some light, a little heat, lots of stink. We never run out of beer, though, right Pop?"

The old man nodded ever so slightly, and if Linc hadn't waved the bottle in his direction, I'm not sure if the old man would have moved at all the whole time we were in there. Wrapped in a blanket and sunken into the deep arm chair, he looked like a mummy.

"It's early," Linc said. "Let's go, I got something to show you."

I heard the Squaw Dance about the same time I could see a glow, low in the sky at the edge of a mesa. I got the eerie sense of ritual. Linc bumped the truck along toward a crowd milling around a bonfire. Dark figures leaning against the night. Indecipherable talk. Somewhere, a high-pitched chant, and another voice, moaning. Inside a broad, three-sided desert tent, a man lay on a raised platform. That's where I stood in the rear of the encircling men and peered into the fiery hibachi, flames leaping into the spitting intestines pulled from what I hoped was a coyote. I didn't drink much beer, and no one passed a peyote pipe my way. I felt clear-headed as the crystal sky as I stood in the tent and swayed back and forth with the rhythmic chanting.

"You're the only Anglo here," Linc muttered from nearby. "Act natural." When he turned to leave, I followed him.

I loved riding the desert trails by night. The hulking shapes of mesas and towering rock formations cut the horizon into puzzling shadows and played with my imagination.

A team of linguistic experts from Arizona State University was completing a decade-long project of recording the oral traditions of the Navajo into print. Linc wasn't happy with the project, nor the least bit confident that it would help the tribe. More than a few times he cursed the translators and vented his anger at me. "The Navajo is a thousand years of signs and symbols. When you Anglos have made all your translations, the true Navajo will vanish."

I always protested, and sometimes he would temper his anger, but not his point of view. The exchanges made for a strange kind of bonding that must have had to do with the vast emptiness around us and the wind washing through the open windows of the truck.

"You stood under the tent of our decline," he reminded me once, matter-of-fact. "You heard Navajo elders chant for the spirits to heal cancer. Our time has passed. You will remember, some day, that you were there."

As we coursed through the glimmer of a dry desert, I knew I'd never forget the reflection of thousands of tossed bottles, the casual, endless trail of broken glass.

Linc dropped me at the bus depot in Gallup when it came time for me to head home. Shaking hands good-bye, I said I'd be back soon.

He punched me hard on the arm and turned toward his truck. "Not as soon as you think, brother."

"Write," I said.

Before I left I'd intended to hike out into the scrub beyond the fence to look for the ring Patty had flung out into the dark, but I never got around to it. As the Greyhound rolled east, images came together: the ring clinking in the sand, the sky opening above the rock shadows, and the hiss of animal fat above the fire. Would I ever see Patty again?

But it was Linc I really cared about, and in my gut I felt him already gone.

We were halfway across New Mexico. Head bobbing, ass twitching, grappling with the limbo of the bus trip, I looked down from my window seat into the bed of a pick-up as we passed. Three men hunkered against the side panels. One cast an empty bottle overboard. I tried to see into their faces as we cruised by, but no one looked up. I started thinking about the glass corridors marking the reservation, how trails of broken bottles were signs of something untranslatable. I thought of Patty tossing Jimmy's ring away like pitching a bottle into oblivion.

We had a short layover in Santa Rosa and then fumed out toward Tucumcari, the bus chugging to get up to speed. In the middle of that nowhere I jolted from a stupor, surrounded by a ring of Indians, fire gleaming in their eyes. One reached out to me and dropped a rhinestone into my hand. I rubbed my eyes clear of visions — yet a hard little shard of glass drew blood. I closed my fist around it and searched the big distance out the window.

Ganado became a state of mind long ago. I remember being so anxious to get there, and ever since, I've been leery of returning to a place that might not exist. It was lonely for Linc in Ganado; he didn't like riding the night solo. I lost track of him soon after he dropped out of Arizona State to write for a local newspaper. He established a respected byline before alcoholism overtook both him and our sporadic correspondence.

In this upstate New York town where I shop, I like to feed the recycling machines at the Price Chopper. Green, brown and clear glass bottles twirl, bob and crunch magically in hungry augers. When the crisp receipt pops out, I pinch it in my fingers and trek to the cashier for my change. The highways around here are free of litter and lush landscaping shields most of these houses from headlights. Sometimes when I stand in my yard I hear a sound in the dark, and I look up to check the stars, strewn through the sky like broken glass.

 **Gary McLouth** earned the Doctor of Arts in English degree at SUNY Albany and won the President's Distinguished Dissertation Award with his first collection of stories, *Death and Other Frustrations* (1985). *Natural Causes* (2008) and *Do No Harm* (2011) build on the promise of that first collection. Gary recently retired from 23 years of teaching at The College of Saint Rose in Albany, NY. He lives with his wife Providence in Fort Myers, Florida.

Ginny Howsam Friedman lives in Dutchess County. She finds inspiration for her paintings in the colors during the change of seasons as well as the grand vistas and the close-ups of nature. www.ginnyhowsamfriedman.com

George Ulrich has enjoyed a career as a freelance illustrator and children's book author since his graduation from Syracuse University as an art major. He lives with his wife Suzanne in Marblehead, Massachusetts.